ONCE
— UPON A —
RHYME

One Week — Three Lives — Three Deaths — A Lifetime in Limericks

ANTONY L. SARAGAS

ARCHWAY
PUBLISHING

This is a work of fiction. All of the characters, names, incidents,
organizations, and dialogue in this novel are either the products
of the author's imagination or are used fictitiously.

Archway Publishing books may be ordered through booksellers or by contacting:

Archway Publishing
1663 Liberty Drive
Bloomington, IN 47403
www.archwaypublishing.com
844-669-3957

ISBN: 978-1-4808-9419-8 (sc)
ISBN: 978-1-4808-9420-4 (hc)
ISBN: 978 1 4808 9418 1 (e)

Library of Congress Control Number: 2020914925

Print information available on the last page.

Archway Publishing rev. date: 09/08/2020

To the teachers who taught me how to write:

Jane Carroll
David Davies
Alice Gross
Charlotte Nolan

And to the coaches who gave me something to say:

E. R. "Doc" Gray
Gayle Huff
Dave Parks
Tolbert Walker

ACKNOWLEDGMENTS

It is impossible to thank all the people who help you navigate and acquire the life experiences used to write a book. Yet I have to try. I definitely want to start by mentally hugging my children, Ty and Andi, who provide daily motivation to get through anything, and I thank their wonderful mother, Tommie, who raised them so well. I thank my parents, Mary and Takis, and my hometown of Harlan, Kentucky, which provided the initial basis for my worldview. I tip my cap to neighbors like Heather Anderson, Sam Mesaros, and Veronica Reitz, who smile and encourage me daily, even on the little stuff. I then thank my professional colleagues at work: attorneys Meredith Horne, Amy Kimble, Anne Mason, and Alton Stainback; judges John Mason and Constance and Paul Carter; and vocational expert Dr. Don Harrison, each of whom provided advice and editing. The crescendo ends by thanking the best of all, Mary Beth Forester, my best friend, who proved it's always worth it to give the right person the right love at the right time.

Lastly, I must thank the hundreds of kids I have coached and all they taught me. I played youth sports as a kid and then coached over twenty years, and I learned this for sure: nicknames are important. When you give kids nicknames, you give them identities on the team and beyond. You give them importance and establish connections, letting them know you *see* them. In their honor, I used nicknames for several characters in this book, but since that method can make the names a little confusing, I am providing a short index for quick reference. My esteemed and learned colleague Dr. Harrison refers to such as a "dramatis personae." While this term is a little highbrow for me, this same colleague also advised, "When in doubt, always crown." So, fancy it is.

GLOSSARY OF CHARACTER NICKNAMES

Oskie: Dylan, the main character and Hollis's son

D-Tay: Dustin Taylor, also Coach D, and Oskie's best friend

Pookie: Zack Baker, now deceased, Oskie's other childhood best friend

Turbo: Oskie's adopted son and travel team catcher

Boo: Casper Williams, Turbo's best friend and travel team first baseman

A Note from the Author

This book is not about poetry. Though the title "Once upon a Rhyme" and the limericks sprinkled in may lead you to that notion, the poems complement the story and point out the major theme of each chapter.

This book is not about sports. Though many of the characters connect as coaches or teammates, sports provide the backdrop of the characters' evolutions through their lives' challenges.

This book is not about a father or a son, even though it is the story of a man and his recently deceased father. It is a familiar story about family, friendship, community, joy, and loss.

Even though this book takes place entirely in one week, it is about life and living.

We all question the usefulness of our past, the course of our present, and on our more challenging days, the point of our future. We wonder about the significance of our efforts.

— I —

LOST AND FOUND

A good poem puts a picture into verse, leaving the paint wet so one can mix in the meanings and emotions that come to mind. Similarly, a good home stands picturesque in a frame of bricks and mortar, holding memories of life within to provide its message to a visitor long after the structure withers.

Those memories were now almost all that remained of 207 North Second Street. Oskie knew that as he climbed the creaking steps onto the front porch of the empty house. The creaking was well deserved for a house after years of wear, a house that had evolved during Oskie's life from his childhood wonderland to its present form as the emotional repository of both Oskie and his father, Hollis, who had died less than a month ago.

It was early February now, Super Bowl Sunday, and Oskie through his frozen breath spied Turbo in the yard. A usually vibrant ten-year-old, impervious to the cold, Turbo had found a stray football and was imitating a Hail Mary in his favorite Philadelphia Eagles T-shirt. The sight took Oskie back thirty years—a happy journey to a childhood of backyard football games, fox-and-hound bike rides around town, and countless whiffle balls lost over the fence into the neighbors' overhanging trees. Hollis had been the losing pitcher on many of those home runs, proudly going next door to retrieve the souvenirs only to serve them up for Oskie to smack again. Turbo would be fine in that same yard, leaving Oskie to procrastinate no longer. He stamped his feet, breathed deeply into his hands—in part

varm them and in part to sturdy his resolve—and then opened the
.reen door and slipped inside.

The first thing you notice in a house without life is the smell. It is
neither rank nor pungent, not offensive, but it is—like the loved ones
left behind—a bit bewildering. It is a smell of limbo, a sweetness of the
past mixed with the stale of the present. Oskie exhaled the smell but not
the limbo. He missed his dad. Glancing around the living room, Oskie
found the second thing you notice in a home now devoid of its master:
a museum of memories. It's as if the home is bragging to a visitor, still
expecting its absent owner to return, almost like a steadfast puppy who
hopes every person who steps through the door is the right one.

Oskie stepped around the coffee table and perused the shelves,
and a lifetime of waves began to hit the shore of his mind one by one.
Hollis had reached the tallest peaks and deepest valleys during his
seventy-six years in that little town. Perhaps he earned both those
highs and lows; no one could say Hollis hadn't lived. Oskie, like many
in the newer generations, had hundreds of instantly snapped pics on
his phones and had long questioned the point of recording memories.
Perhaps the theory is that time moves so fast now that there's little
point in marking it. Or perhaps when you can see and know everything,
there's no point in keeping or caring about anything. But as Oskie
fingered the shelves full of hardware, saved newspapers, and stacks of
photo albums down below, he was grateful for these connections, these
proofs of life. Hollis had lived. He had loved. And his spirit had added
good to the world. He deserved not to vanish quietly, as Oskie used
to think the guaranteed fate of everyone, but for his story to be told.

Turbo let the screen door slam as he entered, breathing hard from
the cold. "Hey, Dad, you think I could get a drink of water?"

Oskie smiled at his son's cautiousness, his vision a bit misty. Turbo
would never have felt the need to ask for food or drink at Hollis's house.
In fact, Hollis would have told him to "shush!" and to get whatever he
needed. Seemed Turbo was in limbo, too, still trying to navigate the
loss of his grandfather.

"Of course. There are glasses in the kitchen. Just don't make a
mess, okay? The folks who want to buy the place are coming by later."

Turbo moved toward the back of the house, and Oskie's watery eyes
returned to the shelves. Growing up, whenever Oskie had contemplated
his father, he had always felt a flood of pride in all his dad had done.
There wasn't much Hollis hadn't tried, failed, or accomplished there
in Wilmington, but it was only a few years ago that Oskie realized the

best stories and deepest scars accrued by Hollis had come from the love of his son.

Oskie's eyes steadied momentarily on his dad's shelf of coaching awards, which had been thinned out to a couple of rows of trophies, plaques, and team pictures dating back a half century to even before Oskie had been born. Hollis had made his money as an attorney and then district judge in Wilmington, and he still toiled as the town's main arbiter of justice right up to last spring. But his fifty years in the law were but moons to the twenty-five-year planet of Hollis's real passion: coaching youth and high school football and baseball. Over the years, his colleagues at bar association dinner parties and the wise men at the barber shop (gossiping codgers dodging their wives' "honey do" lists while drinking coffee and solving the world's problems—everyone's but theirs, that is) would wonder about his passion. Why would an intelligent, personable guy with a law degree return to a small, decaying town to start a new career? And once there, why would he spend the bulk of his energy building youth sports teams instead of taking on profitable cases?

Perhaps it was expert planning on Hollis's part, since Wilmington offered an abundance of kids in need and an impoverished school system that lacked proper staffing. Perhaps it was the complete absence of planning, since Hollis had surely failed to strike it rich as a lawyer, bouncing from private practice to prosecutor to government bureaucrat, making sure any job allowed evenings and weekends free for games and practices. Regardless, while an outsider would see a waste of talent, Oskie had grown up getting to see his real dad through the coaching, not the mask he had worn to feed the family and please everyone else. And wasn't that the point of passion? The strength of emotion displayed even to the chagrin of reason?

"Is that you, Dad?"

Turbo had crept in under Oskie's wing and was pointing to the picture centered in the trophy case. Even though the picture was center stage and purposefully set off from all the other nostalgic mementos, Oskie had yet to allow his eyes to enjoy it. It was like the last piece of corner cake—the one with all the icing that would be the sweetest and last the longest. Oskie knew the picture well. And like all pictures, it was beloved because it never changed, even while the people in it did. It depicted the best team he had ever played on, the best Hollis had ever coached, and undoubtedly their collective favorite.

"Were those your friends?" Turbo's innocent curiosity persisted, as did Oskie's battle to hold back tears.

, sir," Oskie whispered. Even a ten-year-old boy gets a "sir,"
many habits gleaned from growing up with Hollis. "Those were
,y friends when I was your age, Turbo. Grandpa was the coach."

"Were y'all any good?" Turbo glanced up with a teasing smile,
almost as if he knew his dad needed a laugh.

Oskie shot him side-eye back as if to say, *Please ... you need to ask?*
Competition embedded itself in a sports family, even at an early age.
Everyone wanted to run the fastest or jump the highest, have the dirtiest
uniform or give the best sarcastic poke, even eat the most cereal—there
was a scoreboard for everything. Each person wanted to win and loved
playing, even playing at love itself. Hollis had often told Oskie that he
wanted to beat all the other dads in the world at loving his children,
the "love Olympics," he called it, even if it was just an informal game
inside his mind.

"There's some of my old toys and games in the attic," Oskie said.
You ever been up there?"

Oskie squeezed Turbo in a side hug and released him. As Turbo
looked for the attic door, Oskie let himself devour the picture a few
more moments. A multitude of memories screamed from each face,
all dirty, sweaty, and most of all happy from another day in the sun.
Where else would a ten-year-old kid rather be than with his friends,
playing his favorite game? Teachers think team sports or similar
activities can prevent drug use among children, that an idle mind is
the devil's playground. In reality, the games become the drugs. They
are addiction in its purist form. The thrill of endless adventures with
unknown endings yet with the security blanket of fun and friends—and,
in the best cases, one's dad as the coach—win or lose. That's why kids
can—and will—play all day, then gleefully do it again tomorrow. One's
pop psychology magazine may say one can overdo sports with kids.
Oskie clearly disagreed, even thirty years later.

"Dad! Are you comin'?"

Turbo had found the hatch to the attic above the kitchen. "Roger
that! On the way!"

Oskie stopped for one last breath of the past. He inhaled each
face in the picture, each known by the nicknames Hollis had happily
given all his players, such that they became forever known by those
instead of their real names. Oskie had been Dylan before his days on
the team, before some random Saturday-morning practice when Hollis
had christened him Oskie. It was short for Oscar the Grouch on Sesame
Street, an ironic response to Oskie's constant sweaty smile, which

stayed on his face even when he strapped on catcher's gear in the dirt and wet grass at seven o'clock in the morning. There was a backstory to all Hollis's assigned nicknames, and like with a good tattoo, it was the underlying meaning of a nickname that mattered and made it cool.

Oskie loved that photo, even more than he had ever told Hollis and even more than he had ever admitted to himself. He remembered the smiling, but rare was he the center-stage ham as in the pic—arms spread and leaning back into the pile of ten other giggling faces. They had won some game or knew they were about to or had created a new comical memory or knew they were about to. Even better were the two most recognizable faces directly behind Oskie, faces ever so happy as they were catching him in a Nestea plunge, just with a Gatorade instead. Pookie and D-Tay had been Oskie's best friends back then, and the threesome had formed the favored nucleus of what became Hollis's best and favorite team. That team and the trio at its center had been Hollis's corner piece of cake too.

Hollis would have loved that bunch for its sweetness and just because kids were the kryptonite his heart couldn't resist, but that team was also his most skilled. In fact, that ten- and eleven-year-old group ransacked the countryside that summer, going from tourney to tourney and from town to town and even state to state every weekend, and winning so much that Hollis was later recognized as the National Youth Coach of the Year. Oskie's eyes trailed upward from the pic to the display's centerpiece trophy, clearly Hollis's most treasured coaching memory, not because he cared about the silly piece of crystal on the shelf but because it was tangible recognition of how good that team, how good his kids, had become. Oskie's mind flashed to the fruits of that season and award, which had included a trip to ESPN and Disney World. From a ten-year-old's random images, there were Major League Hall of Famers in the room, autographs, and pictures after dinner; and Hollis nervously throwing out the first pitch the next spring on opening day, after which he would simply say he hoped he had made the family proud. Oskie stepped back and wiped his tears, hoping for a full view of Hollis's history and much of his own childhood. Sure, they would gather all these items for storage as the house sold, but they'd never be displayed in this manner by Hollis's hand, and Oskie longed to savor the memory, at least a few more seconds of it.

"Did you play with this, Dad?" Turbo immediately found the portable whiffle ball batting practice machine Oskie had honed his skills on in the backyard thirty years ago.

"You already know, my man ... most all this stuff was me and Grandpa every day after school," Oskie boasted back.

Turbo set about trying to get the electric machine to work in the old attic without electrical outlets, so he quickly resorted to tossing and swinging at the plastic balls manually, smacking them against the decaying attic walls. Oskie found an old rocker in the corner by the lone window, and after a few swings of his own to clear some dust and cobwebs, he fondly remembered the comfort of the chair his grandmother, Hollis's mom, had once used to rock him to sleep.

"Okay if I set this up?" Turbo wanted to erect the old Little Tykes basketball goal ... only about five feet high and ripe for a ten-year-old dunk contest.

"Just don't whine when I beat you. I owned that thing back in the day."

Oskie was kidding but maybe not. Family competition never ended, even for a forty-year-old man against his ten-year-old in a stale, dusty attic. There was always fun to be had, especially since Oskie had adopted Turbo two years earlier; the kidding and lightheartedness were rampant between the two of them.

Turbo proceeded to perfect a few dunks, while Oskie fingered through some boxes and stacks of books along the wall. He knew there would be time to thoroughly reminisce about his dad's life, but for now, with the realtor on the way, he would settle for a quick perusal while shuffling through a series of photos, saved newspaper articles, and heavily worn novels. Highlights included a few action shots of Hollis hugging or high-fiving Oskie after big plays or wins, both during his Little League baseball days and later as a high school quarterback. There were headlines tracking Oskie's All-State senior season, and there were several snaps of Oskie's Mom, Annie, screaming and smiling from the stands, complete with every bit of team gear her body could hold. She was always the loudest, yet endearingly so, and she would never be outdone in her arts, crafts, cowbells, or body paint as needed. Yes, moms in the stands competed too.

At the back of a stack of frames was a portrait of Hollis in his judicial robe later in life, maybe around the age of fifty, after Annie had died and his coaching days had ended. He had risen through the ranks as a prosecutor, and from his grin in the pic, he seemed content with the achievement, but even though the town had revered him as judge, he never quite rediscovered the color of life created from coaching. Maybe it was the combination of change and loss—coaching, Annie, Oskie, and the favorite crew growing up and moving on—but Hollis just seemed a little lost as his beard and then hair turned gray. Not sad and forever a friendly smile to everyone but still a bit of a ghost of his former self, a spirit anxious yet unable to find a comfortable place.

Oskie tried to dodge a couple of wistful thoughts, typical bee stings of any child who lost a parent. *Did I visit and help him enough?* He turned to admire Turbo's crashing reverse dunk, which toppled the tattered plastic goal once again. *Did he know he was loved?* He averted his eyes to the window to spy a passing car. *Did he know he was my hero?*

He rifled his way through a box of books. Hollis was scrupulous in thinning the herd of clutter each year, carting any extraneous clothing or books to Goodwill, so only his true favorites remained. Mitch Albom's *The Timekeeper* and Jeffrey Marx's *A Season of Life* were examples. As in those books, nothing appealed to Hollis more as a coach than the OCD addiction of soaking up every possible second of usefulness and capitalizing on the games to inject life lessons in his players. "That's why you go!" Hollis had been fond of saying. Every practice, every game, every opponent, every minute was an opportunity for something great to happen. So you had to constantly prepare and stay vigilant.

And following Hollis's teachings, Oskie turned over every book in the box, finally hitting a leather-covered journal at the bottom he had failed to recognize. He unclasped the cover to find the following on the first page:

[Journal Page 1]

Limericks, like all of life, are built for smiles and laughs,
But they've lessons built in from all your falls and gaffes.

They can sting you yet also soothe,
They can still you yet also move.

You need both in your heart, held in two equal halves.

Oskie's melancholy shot to more sweet than bitter at that moment. Hands trembling, he managed to thumb the pages of what appeared to be a diary of limericks he had never seen. How had he never known his father was a poet? The sounds of Turbo's thunderous dunks went mute. Oskie sat back down in the rocker and began to read, eagerly searching for and devouring any new part of his father he could possibly find … suddenly full of hope that he could answer the most pressing question asked by a child when a parent departs:

"How can I hang on to them?"

— 2 —

Home Is Here

"Whatcha reading?"

Turbo had no idea that wasn't exactly a soup question. He had no idea of the depths of emotions stirred by the book his dad held in his hand. Of course he didn't. He was ten, dripping with sweat, and ever curious but only until the next great adventure presented itself. He leaned in on Oskie's lap, sharing his wet hair and dusty face.

"It's a book Grandpa left," Oskie almost whispered, swallowing hard and flipping the pages. "He wrote these poems."

"Let's read 'em!"

Turbo's glee erased some of Oskie's harder emotions, leaving a smirk, an eye roll, a shaking of the head. They both already knew Oskie would say yes. Like all kids to their parents, a syringe of Turbo's happy spirit cured all ills, and Oskie sought to protect Turbo's indomitable heart, both to nurture the child's joy but also to protect the parent's own miracle cure.

Good parents can never be happier than their saddest child. So picture the parent as a salt shaker to the child as a meal. The parent stands nearby, ready to offer seasoning to enhance the child's life but careful not to drown out the child's own flavor and add unnecessary weight to their soul.

"Let's go downstairs and take a better look." Oskie squeezed Turbo another side hug, this time enjoying a sniff of his post-playtime boyish charm. They left the remnants of Hollis's regurgitated life and descended the attic stairs back to the kitchen, a convenient and necessary pit stop at this point. It was now past two p.m. and more than three hours, about an hour too long, since a ten-year-old boy last ate. Oskie slapped together some peanut butter and jelly crackers, items impervious to and unspoiled by the surrounding sadness. Problem solved.

The twosome ventured into "their" bedroom; Oskie had grown up in it, but Turbo had long since commandeered it as his own during weekend and overnight stays at Grandpa's house. They crawled side by side into the bottom bunk of the old, red, two-tiered bedframe. Turbo knew the drill, having been happily read to sleep by both Oskie and Hollis over the years. Oskie knew the drill from both sides of the bed, the equal-yet-different joy in giving and receiving the stories. The view of the underside of the top bunk instantly sent Oskie back thirty years or more to his mom and dad training him on his favorite classics, such as *Goodnight Moon*, *Are You My Mother?*, and *Ten Apples Up on Top*. Oskie had gotten off to a fast start in school from that foundation, even once reciting all the US presidents from memory at his preschool graduation, trivia absorbed from happy reading games with Hollis and Annie before bed.

Played hard, full belly, a parent's voice … that was the Pythagorean theorem if he had done the math for a child's nap. True to form, it didn't take long for Oskie to notice Turbo's heavy breathing and hand drifting away from its role in supporting his side of the book. They had made it a few poems in, slowed some by questions on words and greater themes that required translation into Turbo terms, nothing that would sting … salt for a ten-year-old, remember? Even without his reading partner, Oskie scanned the next page.

[Journal Page 4]

Children will grow and go beyond any premonition.
No matter, they still always know; call it intuition.

A real love cannot be lost.
A dad never leaves his post.

And like those, home is an irrevocable condition.

Oskie took a deep breath, holding it while he read it again, and then exhaled. He slithered away from Turbo, sliding the pillow gently under his sleeping smile. Still another hour for the realtor to show, so good timing for the rest, and from his peaceful face, you would think Turbo had momentarily forgotten his grandpa was gone. Oskie eased over to the window, the same window he had peeked out as a child, hoping to see the sunshine so all the backyard games of the day were still on. He no longer saw the overcast, cold day it was but rather glowing scenes of his youth. The room and yard were much smaller now, somewhat decayed and splintering, whether the window frames or the fence out back. To an adult mind expanded by the world, the change was inevitable. But to Oskie's childhood self, the vivid memories were inimitable. He had only six years in that house, from birth until first grade, but reentry to such memories came in slow motion, similar to being underwater. In his mind, he had spent a lifetime there.

Slowly disappearing into that former life, in this movie he allowed his mind to see, Oskie noted himself younger and happier than he ever recalled being. He appeared unsoiled, untouched, unchanged; and he wondered whether Hollis had ever been that way, the way he recalled his younger self and the way Turbo was now. In this vivid replay, Hollis raced home from work during the week to play with a three- or four-year-old Oskie. The darkness outside didn't prevent indoor baseball sessions, with Hollis pitching from the couch and Oskie smacking the squishy ball off the windows and walls before circling the bases around the coffee table. Between innings, there was knee football, with Hollis letting himself be slowly taken down by the cackling Oskie just shy of the goal line, the scene complete with Hollis's humming of the old *Monday Night Football* intro tune. This might go on for hours until Oskie was wringing wet with sweat and had to bathe before bed, the pair pausing only for snacks or because their cheeks hurt too much from laughter. Through the thick fog of the visions, Oskie's eyes found Turbo in the bed, and he couldn't restrain a smile. They had enjoyed many of those days too.

Oskie's foot nudged a plastic car sticking out from under the foot of the bed, and his eyes widened at his find. To anyone else, it was just a small rocking car for a toddler, complete with popcorn sound effects on the steering wheel. But with Hollis, Oskie had ridden that car to greatness in their imitations of ESPN's *World's Strongest Man* competitions. Ever the sports addict, Hollis had worked out religiously, a habit Oskie couldn't help but inherit. The osmosis started with watching those old reruns and then recreating homemade versions of the strongman events. In this one, Hollis had tugged at a rope at one end of the house, pulling the car from the other end. Laughing hysterically, a three-year-old Oskie had sat in that car while being dragged across the living room floor again and again and again. He stifled a chuckle and checked that Turbo's eyes were still closed.

Weekends were varied, all-day affairs. But those generally involved sports as well. By the time Oskie reached kindergarten at age five, Hollis had already invested heavy energy in coaching and running various athletic leagues for local kids. Oskie enjoyed countless Saturday hours at various gyms or fields, and though Hollis tried to love and teach them all, Oskie always got the best seat in the house during any huddle, soaking up all the Xs, Os, and time with his dad possible. Those memories were vague flashes of sweaty faces, but they still felt good. No matter our parents or surroundings, we all have an inner voice that knows when things are way off and when they are really right. Whether back then or in his memory now, Oskie's heart heard and felt a happy, childlike shriek.

That world became even better the following year with the birth of Oskie's sister, Belle. There was a lot of big-brother attention to give, offsetting Hollis's absence while working longer hours to save for a larger house. Hollis was even more fun when he got home, instantly drunk on Belle's charm. By the summer after first grade, Oskie had graduated from T-ball and was a budding young catcher on his first team with Hollis, and Belle and Annie were constant front-row spectators. It wasn't a perfect life for a kid, but he could see perfect from there.

Perfection lay just a few miles away, where he could see the new family home under construction in the blossoming Whitemarsh subdivision. All Oskie could see was the basketball court, full-size whiffle ball yard out back, and—oh yeah, if he and his friends got bored or too hot—a swimming pool. There hadn't been even a twinge of sadness toward Whitemarsh until now, in retrospect over thirty years later, as Oskie could now see that creation of their new life required destruction of the old one here on Second Street, which was full of such simple, plastic, car-like pleasures lost in the search for greater ones.

But this really was the stereotypical American dream, complete with the dainty home—a two-story, four-bedroom, two-car garage, pillared-front-porch-on-the-corner-lot cliché. Hollis had taken a better job as a local prosecutor to afford the upgrade, so add him scurrying off to work to fight crime; the adoring, doting Annie making dinner; and the two young kids enjoying the Wilmington equivalent of Neverland Ranch. And Oskie had unknowingly started life at the top of the small-town food chain. They even had the ideal puppy, a miniature schnauzer named Mia, and lived just a bit shy of perfection and the 2.4-kid average in the most recent census.

In those days, at least in Wilmington and most definitely in Whitemarsh, a neighborhood of other attorneys, doctors, dentists, and local factory executives, kids were safe to travel all over town. Oskie made these mental notes in hindsight. All he cared about then was gathering friends, both teammates and opponents, for all the backyard whiffle ball and basketball tournaments he was planning. Having already seen Hollis orchestrate leagues and events for years, even by the age of seven, Oskie already craved the "Joy Juice," as Hollis termed it for his players. This was a take on the old adage "With great power [or talent] comes great responsibility"; Hollis's kid-friendly corollary broke down as "You have to have the juice [or ability] to bring others joy" and "If you have that juice, you are in fact required to share it." It proved a good ice breaker from a coach to a nervous hitter in the on-deck circle. No lessons, no scouting reports at that point, just Hollis flashing a smile with a pat on the back and a simple question. "You got the joy juice today?"

Oskie's juice would later land him in constant leadership roles on various teams for Hollis as catcher, point guard, or quarterback. As a kid, though, he thrived as a backyard umpire, referee, or tourney administrator almost as much as he did as a player. Joy juice or not, it was a little boy modeling his father, and his father loved what he saw. In the days before Instagram, Snapchat, and even *Call of Duty*, Oskie's home leagues or tournaments became the chatter of kids around town, and Hollis gladly helped out by lining and mowing the yard in the form of a baseball diamond or repainting the three-point line as needed. On special occasions, such as Oskie's birthday or the Fourth of July, Hollis even sprang for the Oskie Invitational Tournament T-shirts.

So, every Saturday and Sunday during school and every day in the summers, double-digit kids flocked from other neighborhoods, either by bicycle or by a caravan of moms dropping them off. One group in particular, from nearby Emerling, had an ongoing standing date for Saturdays, literally a gang of kids looking for action by eight a.m.; and action they would find, breaking from the endless games only to cool off with a swim or a group bike ride to the local convenience store for Gatorade and candy. Oskie planned the games, Annie brought out lemonade or ordered pizza throughout the day, and Hollis was around as "Andy Griffith" to diplomatically solve any disputes the kids occasionally couldn't handle themselves. By the end of the day, up to two dozen kids were exhausted, literally filthy from head to toe, and most begged their parents to sleep over or to come back early in the morning.

For over an hour now, Oskie had replayed his early youth, the trance broken only by Turbo rolling over and opening a groggy eye nearby. Oskie walked toward his son, spotting a tilted frame on the wall beside the bed. Of all his other keepsakes, Hollis had matted and framed a tattered and faded orange pocket T-shirt Oskie recognized instantly. It had been his favorite shirt as a kid on those long summer days in the backyard, soft and comfortable, the one he wore every minute when Annie wouldn't make him put it in the washing machine. Plus the orange stood out, as Oskie so often did, perfect for refereeing, umpiring, quarterbacking, all the ways in which Oskie found himself supplying the juice and joy to all his friends.

Sometimes we develop deep affection for otherwise-ordinary things. On its surface, there was absolutely nothing special about that shirt. In this underwater dream of a past world Oskie was reliving, that shirt wasn't fancy like a seahorse or jellyfish, not rare or cool like a whale or a shark. Granted, it wasn't dainty like a minnow, but it would earn no recognizable name at a dinner table, like a catfish or bass. It would just be an ordinary fish or in this case a shirt. But it's the affection and attachment our hearts put on such things that make them special, that make them valuable and worth keeping. It was Oskie's. All those years. And Hollis had kept it. All those years.

Hollis quoted Lombardi on occasion. "We can never attain it [perfection] ... but along the way, we shall catch excellence." Thinking back and still fully immersed in the fog of childhood, Oskie would say that his mind's instant replay proved Lombardi wrong, that perfection had been caught.

— 3 —

FINDING YOUR FAMILY

The doorbell rang, ending the flurry of memories the way a bell stops a flurry of punches at the end of a boxing round. The realtor was a few minutes early. The electric current of the past was replaced by the dimming sunset of the present. Oskie's shoulders flattened as he walked to the bedroom door, like those same boxers walking back to regroup in their respective corners.

"You okay, Turbo?" Oskie double-checked. Turbo's eyes were open but yet to rejoin the world. He nodded back at his dad. "Just come out when you're ready, sir," Oskie reassured. "You know Ms. Baker always brings fun with her."

That wasn't a lie but perhaps not the whole truth. Every kid loved the Linda Baker Oskie had grown up with. How could you not? For if Oskie's young life in the new Whitemarsh house had put him at the top of the food chain, Linda's family wasn't even on the chain. She likely wore the chain around her neck as jewelry. Or perhaps her husband, Jimmy, who had made his fortune running the local Ford dealership, used it to lock the gates to their enormous mansion, which he had built for her and their three kids on a back corner in the Whitemarsh subdivision. A home like that had buoyed the property values nearby, while a kind neighborhood mom like Linda had anchored a kid like Oskie, whom she had taken under her wing as the best friend of her middle son, Pookie. Oskie had found solace on many late nights in Linda's den, playing video games—it was just the original Nintendo with

Super Mario Bros. and *Legend of Zelda* back then—and eating whole sleeves of Chips Ahoy with her and Pookie. She had been a ten-year-old in a grown-up's body, so she was one of them in spirit yet also had backstage access to snacks and games and extended curfew Oskie and Pookie didn't. From ages six to twelve, she was the ultimate cheat code for fun. And from age thirteen through high school graduation, she had become "Aunt Linda," the non-parent adult to whom Oskie could tell anything and get wisdom without judgment.

But as Oskie opened the door to her face behind the screen, he still felt uneasy, a galaxy away from her cozy couch and cookies. Now in her early seventies, she had navigated aging gracefully, still with cheeks Oskie enjoyed kissing as he took her hand and led her inside.

"It's good to see you, Dylan."

Ms. Baker wasn't being overly proper; she was an insider to Oskie, and she knew the real little boy she had helped raise from a pup.

"Yes, ma'am."

Oskie nodded his standard reply, still a bit nervous trying to connect his eyes to hers. She had been a second mother to him, but he hadn't seen her in nearly ten years. She wore navy and dark green, perfectly adorned with pearls around her neck and wrists. She had always been a classy lady, even back when she had the means with Jimmy to show up all the locals if she wanted. That was just never her style, and in many ways she displayed the same sweetness, just filtered through her now-professional persona as a realtor. Her hair was shorter, her face tanned, and she stood with her hands clasped in front of her wide-legged, boyish stance, youthful as always.

"Would love to have seen you more all these years, Dylan." She broke Oskie's visual interrogation, kindly putting words on thoughts he couldn't. He had known the statement was coming but still mumbled some weak schoolboy excuse for not reaching out to her over the years, something between "Has it been that long?" and "You know how it is. Life gets really busy." In his defense, what does one say to a person from a prior lifetime? It had been a wonderful life indeed yet one that ended some twenty years and three funerals ago, the funerals being their only contact since.

"I understand."

She smiled, of course, already knowing his answer beforehand—along with all the angles within his heart—just as she had when he was a boy asleep on her family room couch.

"You've got a big job, I'd say, Dylan, gathering all Hollis's things.

I remember when my parents died. It was like trying to pull down the past and put it in a box."

And with that her voice embraced Oskie and covered him in the fun of yesteryear. Their lives had followed a similar dance pattern of dodging and deflecting trauma since then, perhaps proving that nothing good ends well; else it wouldn't end at all. But then again, with the memories they both still carried, maybe it hadn't really ended.

They began a stroll around the house, discussing its aging pros and cons for the potential buyers. Though the house carried no debt, and Hollis had left Oskie and Belle some financial security otherwise, Linda would ensure that they got the best purchase price possible. The last walk through, with Linda clinging tightly to Oskie's arm as an escort, also put a motherly touch on his swirling thoughts about what to keep of his father and what to let go. But while these necessities of the day proved bitter, they were wholly offset by the sweet of the past they shared.

Linda had a honey pot full of sugary stories. Zack, the name she had assigned her middle son at birth long before Hollis had tabbed him Pookie, had first met Oskie at the backyard whiffle ball sessions in Whitemarsh. He had meandered over curiously one summer afternoon at the age of six, and the twosome became fast friends. Chubby yet still quite athletic, he had rosy cheeks bookending a constant smile on top of a physically imposing frame. He evoked instant affection and connection from Oskie while admiration, and even intimidation, among the rest of herd. He was part Paul Bunyan, part Pillsbury Doughboy.

A few days into their acquaintance, an Emerling boy got in Oskie's face over a safe/out call in the backyard. Those issues were rare, since in the unwritten playground rule book, the pecking order generally follows the talent and charisma of the kids involved. No different from adult males in competitive settings, there are two questions that come to mind: (1) Am I better looking (or do I have a better life or situation)? And (2) can I kick his ass (beat him at whatever game or task involved)? While aging from the preschool sandbox to middle-school playground, to the high school social scene, or to the corporate boardroom, most men always answer both of those notions with a yes. But occasionally, one wolf stands out as the unquestioned leader, and the pack defers. Call it the "joy juice" from Hollis or the "special stuff" if you prefer Michael Jordan's idea in *Space Jam*, but that was Oskie from day one. Still, there was always an occasional skirmish for superiority among kids, and this one lasted about three seconds. Pookie cleared his throat with,

"Pretty sure you were out, man." And suddenly Oskie's Whitemarsh backyard gang had a copilot.

And so began the friendship, the closest either would have from the age of six to twelve, a run of endless sleepovers, laughter, and time that seemed to stand still. Linda recalled hilarity where both boys donned swimming goggles for hours while playing video games. And how the boys would dress up as their favorite movie characters and recite every line without a miss. How the television once began to blink, strangely only when Jimmy went to the bathroom, before she found the television's remote control in the toilet. No explanations for any of these events were ever found nor needed.

By the time Oskie and Pookie turned eight, Hollis was about ten years into his part-time coaching hobby, a passion that had morphed into the Wilmington Boys & Girls Club. With the Club facility opened and dedicated to him and Annie for all their hard work and fundraising, he passed that torch to others, leaving his coaching heart in need of a new home. He had to look no further than his own backyard. Hollis began working with about ten of the regular backyard crew, honing their skills in baseball, basketball, or flag football as the seasons turned. As the group progressed, Hollis started scheduling them for area games or tournaments, and just a taste of that competitive cocaine hooked them all.

Like any addiction, it grew uncontrolled. This obsession was kudzu on an Appalachian mountainside. From one practice a week and one game or tourney a month, the team swelled with sponsors, uniforms, and activities about every other day. Even if at six thirty a.m. before heading off to third grade, Hollis would find them a gym or a field, and the team would get to pack a lesson and laughter in their lunchboxes to start their day. It had gone from cute pack of puppies to full-blown wolf pack, the kind that became a part of each other, a connection the outside kids failed to fully comprehend but knew they wanted. At the nucleus of that team's molecule, hovering close to Hollis, you'd find the proton of Pookie and neutron of Oskie.

It was on the team's weekend travel adventures that Oskie attached himself to Linda, or perhaps it was vice versa. Every team had that one parent who greased the wheels, sponsoring the uniforms, coming through with the group tickets to a Cincinnati Reds game, or having the expansive RV for tailgating before and after the games. Jimmy Baker would never be Jeff Bezos, but he had caught lightning in a bottle in Wilmington and was in the process of turning all those Ford billboards into a small fortune and later successful run for State Senate. Every team also had that one parent who organized all the off-the-field fun, the one who scheduled the pizza and pool parties, who booked the best hotels closest to Kings Island, who glued a whole weekend trip together. Linda never wanted any spotlight; she just loved kids, including her three—Stephen, Zack (Pookie), and Mary Beth—and anything that made them happy.

So for Oskie and Belle too whenever she could tag along, time with the Baker family provided a kid's three basic food groups: gadgets, goodies, and giggles. Want to hop in the RV and ride to the game with Pookie, with the TV and Nintendo? Want to go with Pookie for a pair of the new Ken Griffey cleats or the newest Easton bat? Want some cookies or McDonald's drive-through? How fast does a kid say yes? One might envision *Elf* with Will Farrell's character mesmerized by candy, candy canes, candy corns, and syrup.

For Linda, Oskie offered a deeper sensitivity or intuition than perhaps she saw in her own children. Pookie seemed to like life simple. *See the ball, hit the ball. Get sweaty and dirty. Run. Score. Laugh. Eat.* But Oskie thought deeply, even then, and he posed questions—about religion, divorce, or death—that kept her on her toes. This was even to a comical extent on occasion, such as once when she went to great lengths to find the right words to explain the female menstruation cycle to an eight-year-old Oskie, only to find out he was asking about changing classes when he advanced to middle school, not *that* kind of period. Linda quickly cherished Oskie's spirit and knew his heart filled hers while providing the yin to Pookie's yang. Pookie needed to understand and seek on occasion, and Oskie needed to relax and just enjoy the ice cream sometimes.

Even on the field, the duo balanced each other and the team, like a "Weeble" that wobbles side to side but will not fall down. Oskie caught and batted second, the quintessential contact hitter who always could move the runner over or lay down a bunt. He led the team in batting average, and he struck out only about once a summer. Pookie pitched and batted third, right behind Oskie, and he was the team's slugger, a guaranteed hit in the clutch. He led the team in home runs, and he frowned only about once a summer—if the team ran out of pizza. In 1990s Hall of Fame terms, and recognizing they were just kids growing into their roles over a six-year span, the team had its Tony Gwynn followed by Frank Thomas. If you prefer a more historical reference, it was the unshakable Lou Gehrig and the unbelievable Babe Ruth. Hollis's job filling in the gaps around them was easy.

Linda and Oskie had relived and recycled these smiles while surveying the house, and they circled back toward the front, when Turbo poked out his head like a turtle from inside the dusky bedroom door. Linda startled, then chuckled, and Oskie smiled too, conceding that in their fun they had forgotten the lad.

"Welcome back, sir," Oskie chimed. "You fall back asleep?"

Turbo shrugged gangly. He was either sheepish from sleep or from the new arrival in the room.

"Come out and say hi to Ms. Linda. She's helping us sell Grandpa's house."

Turbo sized Linda up a second, but he knew well she was friend, not foe.

"Knock, knock," he called to her.

"Who's there?" she replied.

"Nobody"

"Nobody who?"

And there was no reply as he grinned and slithered back into his room.

Linda and Oskie met with their eyes before meeting with their laughter. Forgetting Turbo in the room reminded her of another childhood tale. Oskie had made many trips with the Bakers beyond sports, often finding himself invited to vacations (they had a second home in Florida) and University of Kentucky sporting events (they had season tickets). On one such early Florida trip, with Belle along too, Jimmy and Linda had walked down to the beach for the sunrise, leaving one-year-old Belle asleep and the other kids—their three and Oskie—with video games and cereal. The kids ultimately ventured outside, and a six-year-old Oskie unknowingly locked everyone out of the house, with the exception of Belle asleep inside. The kids ran in fear to find the adults, all except Pookie, and when the frantic family scrambled back to the house, they found Pookie, who had somehow managed to rip the garage door open, literally pulling the doorknob from its socket. He was already inside, finishing his cereal beside Belle so she wouldn't be scared upon waking up. It was that story that officially earned Zack the "Pookie" moniker from Hollis, as in Pookie Bear, an endearing, ever-smiling, yet super-strong and protective Care Bear.

That story had gotten them back to the living room, with Linda putting a checklist of minor repairs in the notes on her phone, as Turbo reappeared.

"I like this one best, Dad. Is Pookie your friend?"

He offered up the open limerick book, and Oskie surprised himself, trying to quickly close it up. Perhaps it was part of a selfish urge to keep the treasure to himself, but it was more the urge not to reopen Linda's wounds, the ones he had tiptoed around since she walked in.

"That's a book from Hollis? Care if I take a look? I promise, Dylan, it's okay." She gently turned the book from Turbo's grip to hers and read aloud.

[Journal Page 7]

Love is given, not received, the strongest of hearts always know.
They are driven and conceived to protect others as they grow.

It's not a Pookie's home run power or trot,
But it is the love for others that they've got.

And in heaven, they're retrieved as they get to reap what they sow.

The two of them both knew the opening line, "Love is given, not received," which was Hollis's pared-down version of his favorite prayer, the Prayer of St. Francis of Assisi. Particularly, Hollis adhered to and tried to teach the kids the basic principle of that prayer, to console, love, and understand others more than needing and wanting those things in return.

Of course, the two of them also knew Pookie. Linda trembled, and Oskie could scarcely watch her face. It was the strangest of smiles, one of pain and conflict smeared across a bright and yet insincere mask, the kind of mask a parent hides behind to survive the loss of a child. It had been ten years of a mask, one she had worn to bury her son, one she had worn through a numb, broken marriage and divorce in the aftermath, one she had worn to start a new career and trudge on as a parent to her two other kids thereafter. But as she looked up at the team picture on the shelf, Hollis's favorite with Pookie holding Oskie up, smiling and surrounded by joy, her mask no longer held. She found Oskie's shoulder and sobbed.

"Promise I'll text you later if we get a nibble on the house, Dylan. You go feed this young man."

Ms. Baker had momentarily turned in tears toward the window and then returned to face Turbo with a comforting smile, kneeling to give him one of her trademark hugs. Like Superman emerging from a phone booth, the motherly hero in Ms. Baker had returned.

"Yep, yep! Dad said we're going to Newberry's!"

Turbo had taken the energy of her hug and morphed it from melancholy to moxie, instantly reframing himself on the prospect of food and fun. Yes, in that way ten-year-olds are superheroes too. He tugged down his beanie over his ears and skipped out the door, zipping his coat as he went. Oskie and Linda stood agape at his exit and then shared a giggle, conceding that Turbo had successfully fractured their frowns. Oskie reached for his own coat and made sure his newly treasured book of limericks was securely in tow.

"I love you, Dylan."

She froze him with those four words, as she had done so many times long before Oskie had grown into his beard and size-thirteen boots. Love had no respect for age, and she knew he needed to hear it now just as he had decades before. She took the opportunity to move in for a hug and kiss on the cheek.

Oskie stiffened slightly, his body and mind still arguing anxiously with affection even as his whole heart agreed. Just like blocking out for a rebound or form-tackling a running back, hugs and kisses require repetition for the necessary comfort and courage, since all physical contact transfers energy. The giver must summon the power and will to initiate, and the recipient must determine how much electricity he or she wishes to accept, in effect how much he or she wishes to be moved. Hollis had always regretted not having hugs on the family practice schedule nearly enough, and he had watched Oskie long struggle to "feel" daring enough to give them or deserved enough to receive. Oskie knew he loved Aunt Linda right back, but he could manage only his customarily muffled, "You too."

"And you tell Dustin and Mary Beth when you see them that I love them too."

Linda softly stilled Oskie's face with her hands, hoping to see the child's heart she knew. "Yes, ma'am," he said, his voice quaking. "You know I will."

She caught a glimpse of the real him just before he nodded humbly, averted his eyes, and broke her embrace to leave. Oskie dodged emotion as a rule, but he definitely could take no more love from her, not from the mother of the best friend he had failed to save, at least not today. He still longed for a glance of the real her, though, and he stopped at the door while eyeballing Turbo in the front yard.

"I trust you on the house, Aunt Linda. I could always trust you with anything." Ten years post Pookie, he managed to leave the "I'm sorry" unsaid, though he forever hoped she understood.

— 4 —

LOVE IS EASY (LIFE IS HARD)

"Hey now!"

Thus began most any conversation with D-Tay, his homemade version of "Say Hey!" from Willie Mays or Jackie Robinson or any hero of yesteryear he had hoped to be at some point.

"Coach Deeeeeeeeeeee!"

And Turbo was off and running in response, past the Newberry's double-door entry, between the barstools and booths of the old-fashioned drug store diner, to the back table—the place's only table, anchored as on every Sunday evening by a smiling Dustin Taylor. He was D-Tay after Hollis had finished naming him, and he had remained Oskie's teammate, best friend, and now fellow high school football coach going back thirty years. Even before that old "corner cake" team took flight, beginning with his initial "Hey Now" as he stepped in the dugout for his first Saturday-morning practice for Hollis, D-Tay's personality was built for instant intoxication. Abstinence wasn't an option. In fact, everything about D-Tay was fast, which is what initially caught Hollis's eye at the Boys & Girls Club, earning him the shortened nickname when Hollis decreed Dustin "far too fast for four syllables." But it was his positivity, no matter the obstacles, that had caught Hollis's heart.

In D-Tay, Hollis saw a fast, tough, fearless kid unaffected by his position in the Wilmington food chain, even though he was several rungs below where Hollis and the Bakers had pulled Oskie and Pookie. Even better, though he waited every morning for Hollis to pick him up from the head of the Fairview housing projects, literally on the "wrong side of the tracks," which ran along the highway and separated him from the Boys & Girls Club and our baseball park, D-Tay appeared unaware there even was a food chain.

"They can't catch me."

Initially, that was D-Tay's stock reply to about any question.

"You ready to play today, D?"

"Need a ride home?"

"Wanna come over after practice?"

"All okay at school?"

Didn't really matter. D-Tay's speed and resolve to outrun any problem were the fortress around his psyche. You'd get a distant stare, his personal guarantee, and then a "What's going on with you?" He quickly flipped any light away from himself. Even at age eight, unbeknownst to his new pals, D-Tay had mastered the art of deflection, because his truth was just way too heavy to carry. Oskie and Pookie just knew he was unafraid of anything, and on any playground or field or court anywhere in a little kid's world, that was just cool.

Of course, Hollis knew of D-Tay's own little personal purgatory, the home life he eagerly exchanged for any practice or game or activity coming and going. Hollis loved the free market of kids and sports, the osmosis of both skills and ideas that passed between teammates in every dugout, car ride, and post-game meal. And he knew D-Tay could use a different perspective on his young life just as much as Oskie, Pookie, and the others could use a dose of his life experience, which you couldn't teach from a book or practice sermon.

To his teammates, the fuel behind D-Tay's white-hot flame was irrelevant; the kids just saw him as their hilarious leadoff man and the hottest ticket in town. He sprinted from the dugout, ready to roam centerfield or scorch the base paths. No one packed the presence or punch to rattle opposing pitchers like D-Tay, who could bunt and steal his way to a triple, even while giggling into his popup slide, or turn a double down the line into an inside-the-park homerun, even while turning off the jets as he rounded third. And so to Oskie's portrayal as Gwynn and Pookie's role as Thomas, Hollis had now added his Rickey Henderson. Or if you prefer the Gehrig and Ruth comparison, the team now had its Ty Cobb. To this day, you could color him part confidence, still yet to be outdone by any player or coach, part underdog, still anxious to show off to disbelievers—even young pups like Turbo who may challenge ol'

Coach D at practice—and the largest part unbridled joy, still wearing that constant smile and enthusiasm across the table from Oskie now.

"We having the usual, big man?"

D-Tay had a way of making everyone feel larger than he or she was, and he knew Turbo's answer just as much as Turbo knew he didn't need to say it. The threesome had been meeting for the same Sunday dinner at Newberry's since celebrating Turbo's finalized adoption two years prior. Oskie and D would talk practice plans and game planning for the coming week of coaching, and Turbo still enjoyed scouring the basket of trading cards or playing video games in the back of the store. No, D's question was only to signal the start of their goofy, grinning contest until the real competition—eating—commenced shortly.

"You two must really be special for me to pass up the first half of the Super Bowl." D-Tay sat back and cockily stroked his scruffy chin.

"Shush, sir!"

Oskie shook off D's sarcasm with his own, mixing his grandmother's favorite rebuke and his father's insistence on respect. "Everyone knows you wouldn't pass up a free meal, even for a big game. You shared with me all those years, remember?"

D-Tay rolled his eyes, but he admitted defeat while patting his forty-year-old expanding tummy. He recognized he was now loose in the cage, an athlete's description for their aging, softening core. He also remembered sneaking out of the dugout on many long, sunny days, using his speed to race across town to Dairy Queen and back before three outs were made.

"You buy, I fly."

D-Tay offered the familiar refrain as a truce, extending the fist bump of friendship, which Oskie would always accept, just as when Oskie bummed money from Annie back in the day, enough to buy both boys burgers and fries in exchange for D supplying the footspeed. He would usually get an ice cream on top for a tip, devoured well before he returned with the bag of burgers hidden in his glove.

"Totchos!"

Turbo was howling and reaching before the plate hit the table, and the race was on. Turbo and D-Tay, both now aged ten in spirit, grabbed and shoveled at a plate full of Newberry's specialty, a heaping helping of tater tots laced with ground beef, cheese, tomatoes, and salsa. The weekly meal then topped off with a round of burgers and chocolate shakes, the real ones people can get only at an aging diner like Newberry's—the ones so thick people were mad at the clogged straw until they were genuinely twice as sad when it wasn't clogged anymore.

"Laverne, could we get another plate of Totchos please?"

Totchos were momentarily interrupted by the voice of D-Tay's angel, the former Mary Beth Baker, the youngest daughter of Linda and younger sister of Pookie. She touched Turbo on the shoulder, then snuggled into D-Tay's lap and circled in under his chin with her cute little trademark "Hi" and a kiss. Oskie had been their best nan ten years earlier but was still left to do a double take, eternally taken aback at her shifts of life, starting from wacky team water girl with Belle at age five, through the annoying little sister phase, then becoming a star high school and college tennis player in her own right before eventually returning as the guidance counselor at Wilmington High.

Somewhere in there she became beautiful, or more likely she just always was. Even as she wiped her runny nose from the cold while covered in a turtleneck, a Patriots football jersey, and a knit skullcap, she drew your eyes curious … tight but tenacious, not dainty yet demure, both salty and sweet. She hung on D-Tay like a koala on her favorite tree. She fit within him perfectly. And D-Tay's face, knowing he had found his unicorn, said "happy," leaving Oskie to count himself 99 percent grateful Mary Beth had captured his best friend's heart, and 1 percent wistful she hadn't stolen his.

"Hello, sunshine."

Laverne confounded the table a bit as she set the refill of Totchos and the check on the table. The Newberry's ambiance was far from romantic, but Laverne was long in the tooth, knew love when she saw it, and she always spoke her mind.

"Lawl, would you look at you two, with the smiles, the cuddling, and the matching jerseys … y'all sure make love look easy. That's good, because it is. It's the life part that's hard. Careful you don't let life get in the way."

The oblivious Turbo was already wrist deep in the second plate of tots, while the three grownups paused to ponder the common sense just spit at them by their sudden milkshake- making philosopher.

"Children …"

She sighed at the blank faces, shook her head, and sauntered away, mumbling disgust at the ongoing silence and apparent ignorance of the younger generation, and in her defense, a common comical debate at Newberry's was whether Laverne predated the century-old café or vice versa.

"Lemme see your book." As Mary Beth reached for Hollis's limericks lying at the edge of Oskie's seat, Oskie slid it over.

"Dad ..."

"Sure, Turbo, you know it's fine."

Turbo was plenty full and had sights on playing his own Super Bowl John Madden style on the big screen at the back of the store. A perk of playing it *during* the actual game was that he had the arcade section all to himself. Ordinarily, there would be two dozen kids hanging after school or on the weekends, just as Oskie and D-Tay had done and Hollis a generation before them; just change the games to *Frogger* or *Pac-Man*. They would also get a steady dose of retired teachers and coaches holding court over why this or that game, this or that play, or this or that kid should have ended up differently. As D-Tay tore into the remaining Totchos along with a funny story from practice the week before, Oskie realized they already had the right table and were just a few more gray hairs, pounds, and stories from that same fate.

"Hey, did Hollis write these?"

Mary Beth majored in literature and philosophy, so she hadn't raised her head from the limericks in over twenty minutes. "And did you see this one?"

[Journal Page 11]

You run all day, run through the night, you run until you fall.
You can close your eyes, turn away, pretend you can't hear the call.

But you run the wrong way, D; you must feel the pain.
Your love is what burns, but it's your sun, not the rain,

'Cause the child of adversity can be the most rare and beautiful of all.

Silence again. But this time the gang held back tears and not laughter.

"Hollis! That old ghost!" D-Tay fought back with his deflection superpower. "That's about like him, trying to get me even from the grave." But his voice cracked as he talked to the sky. "Can't catch me, sir."

"You know he'd be proud if he made you cry with a pregame speech."

Oskie chuckled, offering him a lifeline, but he also knew Hollis would have been more proud of that table scene, his children finding joy and sharing it, even better if because of his post-game—or post-life—limerick.

"Speaking of parents, your mom said she loves both of you."

Now Oskie's voice wavered.

"We know, silly." It was Mary Beth and her sarcasm to the emotional rescue.

"She's meeting us at the house to watch the second half of the game. Grab Turbo, and let's go. Just please make him change that God-awful Eagles shirt."

— 5 —

SUPER BOWL SUNDAY

The best memories are part parasite, part pilot fish. To survive long term, they must attach themselves to a smell, a color, or a sound, maybe even a favorite song, like the way Oskie would always associate his last high school football game with the intro to Van Halen's "Dance the Night Away," the tune Pookie had riffed on his bass guitar in the locker room as the team got dressed. In the case of the Baker house, beyond its sprawling beauty, Oskie's recall returned via the sense of taste, and his mouth watered proportionate to the event—and corresponding menu—involved.

On the usual play night, a most ironic site in Wilmington with 80 percent of its citizenry below the federal poverty line, Oskie and D-Tay and maybe one or two others would hang in Pookie's personal playland, complete with wall-sized movie screen, every video game gadget ever invented, and power-controlled, theater-worthy reclining chairs. Or, on the other end of the house, the guys would find Pookie's two-lane indoor bowling alley along with a couple of pinball machines. Linda marked these casual stopovers by popping open Chips Ahoy or a bowl of Reese's Cups. If the fellas had missed dinner and needed real sustenance, she showered her surrogate sons with an array of Pop-Tarts or their choice of cereal in a cup, a cup endlessly refilled with what had to be a fortune spent in gallons of milk.

On weekly or biweekly team nights, Linda stepped up her game, since she might have a dozen or more mates sleeping over, either laughing while sarcastically cutting up highlights of the previous game, a la *Mystery Science Theatre 3000*, or solemnly scouting film of an upcoming opponent on the big screen. Hollis structured such events early on, never missing a chance to train his troops, complete with his own sarcasm via "The Loafer," his aptly nicknamed laser pointer used to highlight a player caught on film giving subpar effort. For those evenings, Linda whipped up her best spaghetti, biscuits and gravy, or a grilled cheese/tomato soup combo ... always enough for everyone but discreetly the respective favorites of her inner circle of Oskie, Pookie, and D-Tay. The trio's reels of reminiscence remained forever linked to Linda's food, and that's why though the players initially came for the coaching, those nights extended long after the teams faded away.

And then there were the special occasions, birthdays, holidays, Super Bowls, or World Series—even the Little League World Series or World Series of Poker—when Linda made her meatballs. She hovered long over hundreds of her lightly breaded and browned, sensationally seasoned, crispy-covered creations. They were the donut holes or the mini Reese's Cups of hamburgers, where the smaller scale permitted the perfect ratio of ingredients. The boys never knew her methods or even asked. As with any special recipe or secret sauce—whether in food or love—your emotions stir you well past "What's this?" And your mind can mutter only, "More?"

"Where are we?"

Turbo's hushed awe said more than any words he could find. Any Wilmington kid would approach the Baker estate with eyes of wonder and a heart of hope that maybe heaven actually exists on earth. Turbo had met Linda around town a couple of times since the adoption, a hi and a hug here and there, but he had never seen her home. The group walked through the back gate and passed the immaculate pool to see Linda opening the French patio doors to greet them. Turbo led the pack, his curious trance and the comfort of Linda now quelling his nervousness from moments ago. Ten-year-olds are always fond of flashy things. She leaned down to his ear, and her whispers of fun flowed straight through to his instinctive, widening grin.

"Froot Loops, please."

Turbo had made his selection before Linda directed him toward the playroom, and Oskie and D-Tay shot each other a stare, then a smile, and then a headshake, both faces nostalgically saying, *Rookie!* Sure, there was no foul in Turbo's choice of cereal, since names like Froot Loops, Apple Jacks, Frosted Flakes, or Cocoa Pebbles have all stood the test of time in holding a niche within the ten-year-old demographic. Oskie and D-Tay had undoubtedly held down that fort of affection in this same house just a generation before. Linda would likely even break out Oskie's favorite Tony the Tiger spoon for Turbo to enjoy. But Oskie and D-Tay had advanced their adult appetites beyond cereal. This was Super Bowl Sunday, and therefore meatballs and the aroma of the day were open and obvious.

"So glad you're all here. Third quarter just started."

Linda verbal welcome accompanied a peck to the cheek of each guest as they passed into the living room.

"Eagles up three, and both teams might score fifty. Really fun game so far. Catch me up in a minute. The meatballs are almost ready."

She had lived life as a sports mom, so she would have never parted from a good game without good cause, but feeding her children or their teams—all of them—trumped that. She scurried to the kitchen, a smiling hen happy to correctly count all her remaining eggs in the nest under her.

"Well ... look at the three Brady groupies, why don't ya." A new sound of sarcasm entered the room. "I didn't see the bandwagon pull up outside."

Stephen spoke as he thumped down the staircase and bounced in one motion into the living room loveseat in front of the game, mussing Oskie's hair along the way. He fit perfectly, having spent much of his childhood in that position, socked feet hanging over the armrest and chubby in just the right spots to match the cushions now worn and molded to his form. The sofa snuggled him like a pet, almost smiling while absorbing his childlike energy, which belied his mid-forty's face.

"Haters are so unattractive." Mary Beth tossed a pillow at her big brother. "Maybe *that's* why you're single."

"And so is jealousy, sis."

Stephen was always plump and slow afoot but just as assuredly quick of wit. "Not my fault you traded a life of exciting and very diverse romantic encounters for life with your one-trick pony over there." He Frisbeed the pillow toward her and D-Tay, both intertwined on the other couch, getting them both in the face without ever taking his eyes off the game.

"And don't worry, Oskie, I brought extra tissue for when your beloved Brady loses."

Stephen wryly smiled, keeping his eyes on the game and knowing he had now effectively punched all three of them. Oskie, the only former quarterback in the room, already appeared deeply into the game, having idolized Brady for nearly two decades. In fact, Brady's first Super Bowl may have been the last time he enjoyed the Baker hospitality. He simply held up six fingers as his counterargument, covering each of Brady's Super Bowl rings. He also kept his eyes on the screen in defiance, but he knew Stephen had heard him.

"Pretty sure Oskie knows more than you do about good quarterbacks, having been a great one himself." Linda put her words into Stephen's face and laid an empty plate on his lap. "*And you* also know a thing or two about being hated on, don't you?" She pointed those words to Oskie's face, handing him a plate while instinctively protecting her pseudo son even over her own. "Oskie knows I would have watched him over Brady any day ending in Y. He was just as exciting around here." She continued to brag on him as she returned to the meatballs in the kitchen, and Mary Beth crawled out from under D-Tay's arm to go assist.

Oskie held back his smile in typical fashion, still outwardly awkward to such open affection despite her steadfast support for over thirty years. Instinctively, he stifled the scent of such love from family and friends alike, calmly propping his chin in his hands and remaining focused on the task at hand, in this case watching Brady connect for a touchdown that put the Patriots in the lead with just two minutes to go. The "next task" had long become Oskie's learned response to the impossible question. How is one ever worthy of true love and adoration?

Surely Oskie had grown up succeeding at everything, wielding grades, girls, and social graces. He was also the multi-sport star, particularly in football, much to the delight of coaching Hollis and cheering Annie. His star shot more toward football in high school, instantly soaring to fame after leading a comeback and hitting a last second "Hail Mary" pass from fifty yards away to win a game as a freshman. From there, he garnered nine school passing records, multiple All-State selections, and twelve scholarship offers upon graduation.

But even a kid like that doubts his self-worth when his human heart constantly confronts immortal expectations. Perhaps an innate perfectionist spirit, a hatred of losing, is genetic. Or perhaps it's the natural reaction in a family so driven to win. Hollis had been the bridge between his working class, check-to-check immigrant parents and the more comfortable Whitemarsh life he tried to afford Oskie and Belle. But a bridge, no matter how high, can still see from whence it came. Hard work and winning became the cost of never going back. And though never overtly spoken at family dinners or during bedtime reading, Oskie saw that as a kid, hearing Hollis implore him not just to win—that's success—but to positively impact others—that's significance. But instead of enabling happiness, Oskie's childhood actually hardwired him into a contest he couldn't win. Hollis was a beloved judge, coach, and Boys & Girls Club founder from nothing, helping countless families along the way. Oskie saw no path to proportionate significance, considering his life's much better starting position. Hollis's "Joy Juice," the mandate to produce commensurate to your skills, abilities, and circumstances while well-intentioned *coach speak* became pressure, a Jim Jones Kool-Aid condemning Oskie to internal torment. It was perfectionism in overdrive, with anxiety at failing your expected success and guilt for squandering your expected significance.

That's why Oskie had always tensed at pats on the back, why he cared little for all his awards, and why he had ultimately scrapped the idea of further sports in college. What good were all the numbers and awards if the world didn't watch? Where was the tangible impact from the effort? If not Brady-like and setting the world on fire, what's the point of such a façade of success without significance? That's why watching his hero Brady and being reminded by Linda of his own greatness, and being loved for it, were bittersweet.

But that also explained his kindred connection with Linda, why, despite his lack of words, his feet uncontrollably tapped below in response to her affection. Oskie could feign his outer shield of solitude, but inside he allowed his heart to soak in her sweetness. She had always reached him, ably basting his heart with empathy that could come only from a life of her own similar emotional baggage. Both parents—Annie, his spiritual anchor, and now Hollis, his intellectual mentor—were gone, and though long apart from Aunt Linda, he would need her experience now more than ever to ease his angst.

The game clock was ticking down, the Patriots salting away the win, and Oskie was never one to gloat, not even to Stephen, who was ready to change the channel. D-Tay had drifted into a Totchos coma of sleep, and Oskie allowed himself to lean back on the couch and catch a glimpse of Linda through the kitchen doorway. She was exactly as he remembered, not her perfectly polished public persona but the contagiously cute, generously giving mother, her hair up, cooking in oversized sweats and sneakers. Like Oskie, Linda had constantly sought to earn her perceived good fortune, and so acts of service had become her habitually spoken love language.

Linda grew up as one of twelve children in a four-room house at the head of a coal mining camp in Southwest Virginia. Her childhood involved racing her brothers home to be the first to shower, or else the hot water would run out; and each child got one gift for Christmas—a doll without hair or accessories for the girls or a toy truck or car for the boys. Hand-me-down clothes included dresses made from burlap potato sacks, there was no family car, and nightly family entertainment consisted of making mud pies or cutting paper dolls from a year-old celebrity magazine.

As with Oskie, against that childhood backdrop, Linda would never internally earn her later blessings. It wasn't as if she had married for money. Johnny had married her as a blue-collar mechanic, one who learned his craft from age eleven, when he hotwired abandoned cars and used three seat cushions to see over the dash and drive them to the local scrap yard for extra cash. He rose from mechanic to selling refurbished cars, to owning his own Ford dealership, then to having more money than they could have imagined as kids. Back then, she had thought nothing of his money but more of his motorcycle and his cinder-block-sculpted biceps.

Maybe Johnny felt his scrap yard sweat warranted his riches, but Linda struggled to wean herself from her past, caught in a similar circle of anxiety and guilt, that you're inferior and unworthy, and when you fail or are exposed as is destined, it will always be your fault. Of course, this was irrational. No one in Wilmington thought Linda was anything less than regal, but she would never find comfort in her crown. And if your fears and pains weren't real, any attempt to defeat them would always be futile. Linda was constant motion, always cooking and entertaining kids at her house, volunteering at the Boys & Girls Club and Wilmington Humane Society, making sure the team—both players and parents—had everything desired on road trips. But you cannot punch a ghost. Your fist slips right through it. So no matter the temporary pain relief Linda felt from feeling useful to others, no matter the meals cooked, the trees chopped, the stones rolled, the miles covered, she spent years lacking comfort in her own skin. And it was from that life experience that she had drawn wisdom to relate to Oskie growing up, particularly after Annie's premature death when he was only sixteen.

"Hold up!"

Stephen popped up from his mini post-game nap. "Did we ever get meatballs?"

Finally, Oskie couldn't help an outright laugh, since Stephen resembled a Will Farrell character, who would live in his mom's basement, fail to launch, and spend his days yelling for meatloaf and video games. After the emotion of the day, Oskie both needed and deserved the chuckle. Plus, for once, Stephen had a point. It was very unlike Linda not to serve her boys, and all three meandered into the kitchen to investigate. Ten o'clock wasn't too late for three grown men to pillage good food.

Stephen ignored the ladies and followed the smell of meatballs to the stove. D-Tay found Mary Beth sitting at the kitchen table. He softly massaged her neck from behind and kissed her check. Oskie's eyes went to Linda, who was braced against the kitchen counter, her eyes centered on the limerick book, opened to the following:

[Journal Page 15]

You can be their morphing mortar, connect the corners
of their lives' pointed bricks.
You can have an elastic heart, bend and deflect their
pain, shield them any trick.

But your sweat cannot their blessings earn,
Nor your falls be why their bridges burn.

You can't hold up every pillar for kids; a parent can
never be that quick.

"Sorry, we got carried away."

Linda and Mary Beth smiled at Oskie, smiles partly crying not from sadness but from connection. To truly feel the heart of another, even from the grave, is the most tear-worthy human experience.

— 6 —

READY FOR BED

"Had enough, sir?"

Oskie peeked into the game room, finding Turbo still entranced in the John Madden version of the Super Bowl, headset on, laughing with unseen friends from across town or across the planet. There was no difference anymore to kids his age.

"Five minutes?"

Turbo's expected reply defied the technology around him. No matter how perfect, science will never change a kid's desire for extended playtime, to infinity if possible, sleep and the next day of school be damned.

"Deal. But no overtime. CP is waiting."

Oskie had to get Turbo in the bed for the new week of school but also had to get home to give their dog, CP, a needed bathroom break. CP was Oskie's third mini schnauzer following Mia, their family dog while growing up, and Cash, whom he had inherited from Pookie ten years ago. CP was short for "colon parentheses," another Hollis nickname, representing his favorite old school smiley face emoji and also the smile the pup had given to Oskie and Turbo as a gift last Christmas. :)

"I'll meet you out front. Don't forget to thank Ms. Baker."

Oskie bid his own farewell to Linda, gathering the limerick book, her required hug, and his fair share of meatballs for the road. The typical side hug for Mary Beth, a man hug for D-Tay, and a head nod to Stephen. And with one last grateful look at his remaining extended family, he was out the door. Turbo raced through moments later, trading a hug to Linda for a sampling of meatballs, each feeling he or she had gotten the better end of the transaction.

"You gonna be okay for practice in the morning?"

Oskie, like many parents on the way home or to school or to events with their kids, had wasted words. Ever busy and attempting to manage their own stress, parents unknowingly call out to their kids for reassurance. He didn't truly doubt Turbo's lack of sleep affecting his energy or enthusiasm; he was simply second-guessing his decision to let Turbo stay up late on a school night, even though he had known it was the right thing to do just a few hours earlier.

"Da-aaaaad," came Turbo's moan from the back seat. Parents hope for a verbal hug from their child in that moment, but instead the child stiff-arms the perceived nagging. Kids spot nonsense on sight, even as they can't appreciate the reasons for what they see. And no one hugs out of exasperation.

Oskie managed to control any further compulsion to annoy for the three-block trip home across Whitemarsh. They made it inside to the delight of CP, who hopped and squealed until the urge to pee outmatched the urge to be petted. He skipped off the porch to the front yard, while Turbo headed to brush his teeth and get ready for bed. The adrenaline of the day, Hollis's house, Newberry's, the Baker mansion, the Super Bowl, and endless cereal had left fatigue in its wake, the kind of fatigue kids know and feel, no nagging required.

Oskie milled quickly, gathering the team's gear for the morning practice and casting a quick eye to ensure Turbo's glove and bat bag were by the front door too. He climbed the stairs toward Turbo's room, CP bounding before him two steps at a time. The pup paused at the hallway bathroom, pointing at Turbo brushing his teeth. Oskie passed, and Turbo uttered some indiscernible, encumbered, tongue-tied scrubbing sound of a question. The only proper reply was laughter for the three seconds Turbo could hold closed his mouthful of goo and for the full minute after he barely splattered it into the bathroom sink.

Oskie giggled on toward Turbo's bed to turn it down. His feet gripped the carpet in the familiar house he'd grown up in, and he could still pick any of their favorite books from the shelves lining the hall without looking. After Annie's death, Hollis had held on there until Oskie and Belle left for college, but then the size of the house and the memories dwarfed his spirit. Hollis had moved back downtown into the Second Street house, which he had kept as a rental. To Oskie's good fortune, the Whitemarsh home stood empty until his prodigal return for Pookie's funeral ten years ago. Now here he was, in the same house, performing Hollis's same late-night milling and hovering, and ushering both son and schnauzer to sleep just so they could rise early for a ten-year-old travel baseball team to get an hour of gym time for throwing, soft- toss batting practice, and infield grounders before school. Oskie in his twenties may have never even thought of coming back to Wilmington, far less ever want to, but now at forty he had turned into Hollis Jr.

By the time Turbo belly flopped into the sheets, Oskie was already kneeling bedside, and CP already rooted comfortably with eyes dimming into the adjacent pillow. The clock had crossed eleven p.m., and though Oskie cherished those sleepy moments as sacred, as a chance for nightly nourishment between father and son, another of Hollis's hand-me-downs, this wasn't a time for a fireside chat.

"You wanna gimme that again?" Oskie invited Turbo to restate his bathroom question, this time sans toothpaste. He kissed Turbo on the forehead. "Make it quick tonight, sir. You know it's late."

Turbo smiled, eyes heavy and half closed.

"I was asking whether you think I am good as you were when you were age ten. Or Coach D."

"That's not exactly a *soup* question, sir."

Oskie's term came from *Finding Forrester*, a favorite movie of his and Hollis's while growing up, a non-soup question being one that sought information irrelevant to the inquisitor, one not geared to anything useful. In essence, he was politely pointing out that the question was "not your concern" or, if more adamant, "none of your business."

"You know it's always best to be yourself in this world."

Still Oskie smiled when he said it, fully aware that Turbo was hoping himself a future Oskie the same way Oskie had eventually become in part former Hollis. A father cannot help but smile at and share such a dream for his son, and despite the late hour, he would gladly think "outside the bowl" of soup with Turbo on this one.

"Da-aaaaad."

Oskie chuckled at Turbo's sleepy sigh, the proper reply—yet again—to his unnecessary parental qualifier. He knew to just answer the question, but dads and especially coaches never stop planting seeds.

"You're part me *and* D, I think, and likely the best parts of both of us. I was always steady and calm under pressure. And I know Coach D may play around with you, but as a player? He was always the toughest. Showed no fear and gave no breaks. To anyone."

"And you think that's me?"

Even a tired ten-year-old could catch a compliment.

"Can be. It's not that I didn't feel pressure or that Coach D didn't feel fear, but we learned to do our jobs anyway, like you do."

Oskie closed the comment with a second kiss to the head and a tug of the sheets, and Turbo closed his eyes contently, the way anyone can when trust allows him or her to turn off all defenses. Oskie loved the way Turbo could sleep and loved to watch him, feeling lucky to have a son.

"Ya know." Oskie stopped at the doorway, his affection torn between the benefit of Turbo's sleep and planting yet another seed. "You actually resemble my friend Pookie most of all. The way you move and play and even sometimes the way you act. You never got to meet him, but he was our best player."

"What position did he play?" Turbo's lips managed to mumble while his eyelids failed to move.

"Anywhere he wanted. He led, and we followed." Oskie flicked off the light, allowing Turbo's toothy grin to glow in the dark.

Back downstairs, Oskie settled into the living room recliner, where he would often wind down with his thoughts of the day. Single dads sleep in recliners or on sofas, even on the floor, with muted ESPN highlights to wash away the loneliness. Perhaps it was the limerick book in his lap or the now-half-downed bourbon in his hand, but Oskie's mind skipped between memories to beat the coming sleep the way a coin bounces across a pond before finally sinking below.

He pondered his old friend Pookie, he of the dominant talent and personality that Turbo, had he known him, would have idolized like everyone else had. Pookie was modern-day Midas. He never worked out, never studied, and, at least outwardly, never seemed to care to be perfect, yet when it came to grades and games, perfect he was. Only Pookie seemed capable of blowing everything off the night before, then laughing while blowing away the competition the next day. Vintage Pookie called his shot, delivered the home run, tossed the batboy a souvenir, winked at the blushing girls behind the dugout, high-fived the coaches with gratitude, and made the rest of the team feel equal to him in one at bat, even by the age of twelve. His smile was bright and real, and with him teammates stood a little straighter, feeling invincible. His scorebook position said pitcher and catcher, but if you asked him, he "threw smoke and hit dingers"; and if you asked a raving Hollis, Pookie set the example of combining the three necessary bones of any young man: the wishbone (have a vision), the backbone (work hard), and the funny bone (enjoy the ride).

Pookie's big stick and smile had carried their travel team, then his high school team, then the label of Oakland A's draft pick before his ride sadly ended. From that end, Oskie's mind's eye gravitated to Linda, the mother Pookie had left behind; and Annie, the mother Pookie hopefully had gone to find. Oskie had adored Annie, whose surviving spirit via her portrait on the wall easily invaded his mind even after twenty-five years of absence. With her works somewhat hidden in Hollis's shadow, Annie had also given her whole heart, guiding kids to the Boys & Girls Club, counseling clients on mental health, and loving Oskie and Belle before that heart just gave out one afternoon on the way home from work.

Years before Annie's death, a preteen D-Tay had grown close to her. With a faded connection to his own mom, last seen fleeing drug rehab, and his dad, yet to be seen at all, D-Tay's steely resolve matched up with Annie's magnetic strength. He followed her path into counseling and teaching to have a similar impact on others. But she would always be Oskie's mom, always a soothing presence and always an agonizing absence. His thoughts automatically ricocheted from such hurt to the comfort of Linda. Oskie struggled to feel deserving of one good mom, let alone two, but he smiled, knowing he and D-Tay had shared them both.

While Oskie and D-Tay had shared moms, Pookie seemed to shun such mothering from an early age. Children are so eager to meet and experience and be fulfilled by the world that they often run right past their parents. Like running to friends on the school bus and forgetting their backpacks are full of homework, kids see all their wants and are blind to their needs. Fingering the next limerick ... slowly drifting to sleep ... Oskie could blurrily see Hollis walking into fifth- grade homeroom, bringing a forgotten backpack to Oskie's ten-year-old self.

[Journal Page 19]

You look out to a curse of many options, so many impossible choices from where you sit.

Nothing is harder to bear than your freedom; you fear being weightless but still must say yes to it.

And in limbo, a buoy or post for gravity you cannot invent,
So you stay moored to what you know, to your lovers, your friends, and your parents.

Life gives you the path to all your hopes and dreams, but it also takes them away lest you know where you fit.

Whereas Oskie and D-Tay had run into the arms of Linda or Annie, respectively, the group lacked a third mom to complete the boys' sacred hoop and to nab Pookie as he ran off to find his life. Instead, Pookie got mothered by fame, by the flock of followers who cheered but never loved him, raising him up addicted to adoration. As with the latest designer drug, social media platform, or even those first all-night text replies from a new infatuation, each hit or "like" or ding of the phone brings a transient high. Eventually, though, the coke, crowd, or crush subsides, casting the addict afloat without his or her fix, and a hero like Pookie is left hollow.

There was just so much loss to trace that day, Oskie thought. He would be sad about it one day. Maybe he would even cry about it. But tonight he was running on empty and just too tired, and he sank into sleep.

— 7 —

IT'S JUST PRACTICE

Every practice proposed a lesson. A good coach is more than a tactical expert, more than a skilled artisan honing an army of apprentices. The best breathe hope into their players, a larger vision of purpose focused by every word, every laugh, and every drop of sweat. It's that desire to turn a simple kids' game into something more meaningful— the belief that as a group you can create something more than you could ever create alone—that provides a coach and his comrades real, lasting motivation. Those daily life lessons ultimately erect the house known as a "team." The wins and losses come and go, and they are important houseguests to enjoy or learn from, but they enter through a separate door and are never allowed permanent residency. A true team houses only the hearts of its players—its family; each is permitted enough personal space to grow individually, but each is also linked to the others to grow collectively. That makes the coach the home's butler, tailoring the nutrition and instruction to each kid uniquely and ensuring the home's shared Wi-Fi connection between the boys is at full clarity and unity, without interference from the static of jealousy or selfishness.

The message this Monday was always Hollis's favorite word and so engraved on Oskie's heart that he now offered it to Turbo's group as if on autopilot. Hollis had always opened the week hammering in some form on the essential foundational block of empathy. It is empathy, the ability not just to understand but also to actually feel and care about the heart of another, that enables the essential balance in the eternal dichotomy of all sports.

A great player starts from a seed of selfishness. He or she must always want the ball, the last shot, to pitch or bat cleanup, to have the key play called in their direction. Great players crave the limelight; they are willing to sacrifice friends and other interests to work long hours for that individual fame, and because of that sweat-equity investment, they grow easily angered by unequal commitment or perceived incompetence around them. And that intolerance—for mediocrity, for losing, for obstacles and adversaries, and even for your own weaker teammates—is the spur for the extra hours, late nights, workouts, diets, and sacrifices required for individual greatness at anything. The best players want to beat anyone and everyone, any perceived threat, even eat and kill them in a more Mike Tyson moment. Winning requires these kids, so a coach recruits them and releases them throughout the house in hopes that their disease of desire infects the rest.

Hollis was no saint in this regard. He started looking for wins in the morning shortly after breathing and breakfast. He made a game in his mind, himself against the world around him, whether prosecuting in court, playing or coaching at the local gym after work, or parenting at home. Even if only for the silent scoreboard inside his head, Hollis counted everything—cases and verdicts, reps and weights, lessons and wins. There's certain vanity in such thoughts that you can and must beat everyone at everything. But within Hollis's narcissism was also a sense of blue-collar, underdog pride. No one handed him wins; he intended to earn every one of them. He would take on all comers, a chip on his shoulder, even against a world often unaware it had challenged him. Whether he shared Linda Baker's struggle to justify his adult successes or remained enslaved and unable to shed his childhood dreams, Hollis needed to win.

So to win, Hollis sought the necessary players, attracted to their talent but more to their tenacity, the latter being far more scarce and far more valuable. Such was Hollis's life experience. But Hollis's coaching experience had further taught him that the best teams came not from the best *players* but from the best *persons*, and the best persons require empathy, plain and simple. Per Hollis, the only way for one to have purpose and greater impact—no matter how much individual achievement—was through empathy, to truly love and be loved. The emotional skills of love and empathy, though directly opposed to the selfish concept of winning at all costs, were the only effective glue to hold the group together, to elicit "individual commitment to a group effort," as the great Lombardi phrased it. Any group, team, family, community, or even nation belabors this balance. How to get great individuals, ambitiously believing their best performance results in the best for all, to join together to achieve group goals, or to fill the needs of others. It's the "invisible hand" of free market capitalism arm- wrestling the outstretched hand of charity or socialism. Coaches glorify sports as a microcosm of life, but perhaps they mean government or politics. You need capitalism for players to be great but socialism for them to want to do it together as a great team. Too much team socialism results in a lack of killer instinct or performance under pressure, the eternal "nice guy" runner-up. Too much capitalism reflects in a lack of grace and character shown to outsiders in victory or defeat and in inner team turmoil bickering over perceived glory.

Perhaps Hollis thought too deeply about the greater impact of youth sports. Perhaps Hollis should have been president.

"Take a deep breath, boys. Smell the baseball."

Warm-ups complete, skill and drill stations next up. Oskie started practices just as Hollis did. The empathy injections began early and often, even at 6:15 a.m., sprinkled in among each session. Most lads won't sit for a sermon, so like a doc giving kids their weekly allergy shot, this one hardening them against selfishness, a coach hides the needle while focusing them on the joy, on the scents and sounds and scenes of their mates all around them.

"Soak it in, guys. The leather, the sounds, the sweaty, dirty faces of your brothers. You'll remember those faces when you're an old man like me."

True. It was still so easy for Oskie to recall his team of yesteryear, mindful snapshots of D-Tay, Pookie, and the others. Oskie could still vividly recall Pookie's grimy, chubby childhood face, complete with a tennis-ball-size wad of chewing gum in his jaw, staring in from the pitcher's mound to Oskie's catcher's mitt during many a sweltering summer practice. Oskie could see sweat dripping off his catcher's mask and, beyond those droplets, a dusty ten-year-old D-Tay leading off first base, knowing he was going to steal second as surely as Oskie knew he was going to throw him out.

An outsider might question why coaches stay excited and serious about a kids' game, why coaches pack and cart equipment in the cold to an empty gym before six a.m., why fans spend time and travel to sporting events across the land, and why parents taxi their kids and shell out mad money for sports adventures. But an insider knows it's the emotional heroin that brings people back, pain relief and distraction from the hard parts of life. Just as it was described in several of Hollis's limericks, one of which Oskie had skimmed just before the kids filed in for practice.

[Journal Page 23]

I've loved coffee, ice cream, and every kind of M&M,
Legal and wonderful addictions, one and all.

But coaching a good team is better than any of them,
And the lessons learned therein, you'll always recall.

Only a team can bring you both laughs *and* tears,

Then leave you friends and brothers for all the years,

I might cut out the others, make myself healthy and trim,
But I'll always coach whenever they call.

And thus goes the soothing song of a baseball practice, a *ping* marking the beat with each grounder Oskie stroked to the infielders. "Don't let your brothers down now! They're working for you too!" Oskie worked in a verse on sacrificing for each other, whether a bunt hitting to the opposite field to move a runner or getting your body in front of hot ground ball. A *whish* of strings from each swing the players took, cracking soft-toss whiffle balls off the gym walls.

"Don't waste your talents this morning! Everyone else is sleeping in out there! You have a chance to get ahead!" Oskie repeated Hollis's familiar chorus of making use of every opportunity. A *smack* of percussion from every glove around the diamond. "Focus, gentlemen! Make your next throw your best one!" Oskie added the melodic lesson of integrity, to always offer all they had on each play, no matter fatigue or any mistake the play before. If you could wind the world back thirty years, you might have heard Hollis singing the same song with Oskie in the band. And now here was Oskie leading—the laughter, noise, and focus erasing the melancholy of yesterday.

But a slam of the gym door disrupted the dance, and Oskie held the next play, now remembering D-Tay had been strangely late this morning. A fifth-grade math teacher by trade, Coach D might miss a morning travel team practice if he drew bus, cafeteria, or traffic duty, but this wasn't one of those days.

"What's up, fellas?"

D-Tay threw his hand up with a smile, puffing a smoke screen that worked on a team full of distracted kids but not on a best friend. He walked past the group to the lockers, where he might go to change clothes before practice but not while already in shirt and tie with only fifteen minutes left before school. Oskie worried, but he proceeded with the next groundball so the kids wouldn't. He quickly closed up shop for the team, summarized the day's lesson, set the next practice time, and cut the kids loose toward their classrooms. A quick squeeze of Turbo, eyeballing to be sure he had his backpack, and Oskie was off to find his pal.

"All alright, sir?"

Oskie slid open the locker room door to see D-Tay wiping a tear in the mirror.

"Not him. This is *not* supposed to happen to Boo."

D-Tay dry-heaved, holding back further invisible tears with a conflicted face, the one that showed a grown man longing for rescue but at the same time wanting to tough it out and be left alone.

"Where is he now?"

Oskie had feared for Boo, the team's beloved first baseman, who had been noticeably absent for two of the last three practices, including today. But for being the roundest figure on the field and least likely to steal a base, you could attribute every other trait of D-Tay, including his childhood home life, to Boo.

"They've taken him. All of them. I went by to pick him up like always, and they were gone. The place was empty. And no one will tell me anything."

D-Tay gripped a sink as if to rip it from the wall. He saw his tortured face in the mirror and turned away in anger before bending over, hands on his knees, in exasperation.

Christian Casper Williams was the oldest of five brothers, growing up in the same housing project once laying claim to D-Tay. Everything about him was big, most notably his appetite, his toothy grin, and his home run swing. He had instantly been D-Tay's favorite and a no-brainer addition to the team. With his friendly ghost smile and a name like Casper, the nickname Boo was also a no-brainer.

But Boo was far more than just a ride-share partner to Coach D. On those morning and weekend drives together, D-Tay had learned Boo's heart-wrenching story. Boo's mother had disappeared shortly after the birth of Isaac, the last of the five brothers, when Boo was seven. She had long dealt with drug addiction and had a last-known address somewhere in Southern Ohio. Their father, Terrance, was occasionally seen around town, most assuredly drinking from a brown bag. By all accounts he had played little part in the kids' lives, and he was rarely seen at their small two-bedroom apartment. The kids slept two and three to a bed, and thankfully, Terrance's sister, Angie, lived two floors down and had managed to keep the utilities on and leave food for the boys after school. Boo was the man of the house, making sure the younger kids bathed, dressed, caught the bus to school in the morning, shared dinner, did their homework, and didn't quarrel before getting to bed each night. This role for him had gone on for almost two school years, since Terrance's ability to stay out of jail, Angie's assistance with necessities, and D-Tay's cab service to extracurricular activities had delayed potential intervention by local social workers. Clearly, Boo required no further empathy or manhood lessons by the fifth grade, and if D-Tay ever needed an empathy refresher, he would never feel anyone's pain or life more than Boo.

"He's gonna lose his brothers, Oskie. I know what they do. They'll split them all up," D said as he was still dry-heaving in grief. "He's gonna lose his team. He's gonna lose us. He'll be all alone. He's just a kid, Oskie. He needs us!"

D-Tay shivered from the shock of his morning, the frustration of his helplessness, and most of all the memory of his own pain. Oskie knew all too well that D had been similarly shuttled away from his home, his siblings, his teammates, and his beloved Coach Hollis, and into the state's foster care system at age twelve, less than two years after the pinnacle of their childhoods on the "corner cake" team.

Just moments earlier, practice had reminded Oskie that if sports were drugs, he had grown up in the royal palace of crack houses and that he longed to keep that indulgence alive for himself and Turbo. For both coach and player, and father and son, there was the prospect of euphoric and joyful high from creativity, achievement, impact and significance, and longevity.

And now yet again, life reminded him of the frank, cold, come-down clarity no sport-related lesson can save the world or, in this case, just one innocent kid. All empathy does in these moments is help one feel the pain that much deeper. Yes, Hollis's brand of manhood inspired young men to immerse their hearts in others, to feel and share and help, but that also results in tremendous weight to carry against a world already set to spin in the opposite direction. As an adult, Oskie had learned you cannot solve everything or sometimes anything. And he had watched Pookie and D-Tay and eventually Hollis all tumble and fall from that realization. Real life had sobered each of them one by one with pain, breaking each of them free from the fairy tale of those dreams and teams. Oskie had long since numbed himself from the pain, defiantly considering himself enlightened. A realist. He still believed empathy was the best way to motivate and bring a team together, not a bad trait to instill in young men, but he was no longer romantic about it.

"Let me see what I can find out."

Oskie had gone full stoic mode, his means of dodging the hurt. He would promise no miracles, but as Wilmington's only local juvenile justice probation officer, he'd have a chance to pinpoint Boo's status and any possible chance to intervene.

"Please, Oskie. I'm begging you. We can't let this happen."

A knock at the locker room door broke the tension. Oskie cracked it open, finding the smiling face of Turbo, a kid's smile that said, *I'm excited and want to walk to class with Coach D* and not, *I just heard the bad news about Boo through the door.* Oskie and D were both thankful for that. D-Tay discreetly dried his emotion and draped an arm and smile around Turbo, walking him toward the school hallway as Oskie headed for the parking lot.

"Let's go learn something, sir."

Integrity. Another Hollis lesson. Trudge on with your best foot forward always but especially when times are tough. In his words, "anyone can do the right thing when you're winning, but a man provides. He takes care of others, even when the sky is falling."

— 8 —

IGNORANCE AND ARROGANCE

O skie had a lot on his mind as he skated across snowy Wilmington in his silver Toyota pickup, granted only about two miles on his usual post-practice path home to clean up and then get to coffee at the courthouse by 8:30 a.m.

"You again?"

Veronica, Judge Peterson's secretary, "Ronny" to most, always let Oskie in as she opened up the office so long as he could take her adjoined southern drawl and sarcasm. Fumbling for her keys, she propped herself awkwardly on a replaced knee and hip, but otherwise her spirit hadn't aged in the thirty years since Oskie first met her.

"Can't get enough of you, Ms. Veronica. You already know."

Oskie offered a sarcastic grin and wink of his own, his reflexive deflection of kindness, a preference to keep folks on the surface at arm's length. That's why he spent mornings before work with gas station coffee waiting on an empty courthouse bench as opposed to Newberry's Café across the street. Seclusion was better, or so that was the lie Oskie had told himself long enough to live and believe.

"Uh-huh ... still the charmer, I see." Ronny dropped her purse on her desk, snapped on her computer, and started a pot of coffee.

"When did you first use that line on me? Fifth grade?"

That was when she had first met Oskie, at the age of ten. It had been Hollis's office then, a brand-new judge with a brand-new sassy secretary he had snatched from serving coffee at Newberry's. She was a quick study of people and a natural at giving bad or unwanted news with a smile, a sweetness and candor that brought acceptance. She was perfect for protecting the turf of a district judge from a public usually desperate or defiant in their requests, the law be damned.

A childhood Oskie, with his daily courthouse pit stops between classes and practices, became her after-school delight back then. He got a snack and cartoon break on a beanbag in an impromptu playroom Hollis had set up for the kids in the rear of the office. Ronny got to play mom, another role she was perfect for but had never gotten to play. She would have been a permissive parent, so when Hollis limited Oskie to four powdered donuts of the six that came in the pack, just a dad trying to steal a couple of donuts for himself under the guise of good parenting, Ronny would sneak him two of hers. She had sneakily seeped in through Oskie's outer shell ever since.

Ronny rode Hollis's whole career in the courthouse, and she had also tracked Oskie's evolution from light-hearted, clever, hilarious kid to focused, fantastic, high school sports king ... from donuts and afternoon cartoons to cell phones and YouTube videos. At the start, she answered homework questions, packed up sports equipment, and tried to broaden his worldview; and by graduation, she was giving girlfriend advice, passing him cash left by Hollis, and trying to reduce the usual risky behaviors for a teen. For both Oskie and Belle, particularly after Annie died, Hollis had enlisted Ronny as a deputy against the "three Ds"—drugs, debt, and divorce—which can wrest control from and derail a life. Hollis had seen lives everyday mired in years of anguish over drug addiction, debt overload, and departures after marrying the wrong person.

"Yes, you bribe me with coffee and donuts, but that doesn't mean it's not true," Oskie chimed in, making sure to say the right thing. "Big docket today?"

"Nothing you can't handle, sir. You already know."

Her "sir" was a Hollis habit, echoing as a reminder of him around the office, and she sent the "You already know" words right back at Oskie as a deeper reminder of her steadfast faith in him. Just like Hollis and Annie before, Ronny longed for Oskie to share that faith in himself, in his own heart. She knew Oskie's words were now most often from obligation than opportunity.

She also knew she had missed the valley of Oskie's life, flanked by Annie's death before leaving for college and by Pookie's death, which had prompted his return to Wilmington. Somewhere in between, Oskie lost his compass, becoming a man without a country, opting to embrace his detachment as destiny. Ronny kept it light, but she hid her sadness at Oskie in his present form, still kind and considerate to everyone but more as a defensive cover.

Oskie grabbed a coffee and a seat on the office sofa, the beanbag long since relocated. Yet again, he followed the habits of the absent Hollis tacitly, including this twenty minutes before court with caffeine and quiet. Every day since Hollis had steered him toward the juvenile justice gig ten years prior, he used this morning meditation to reset his memory. No matter how many cases you may have closed or how many faces you may have failed, no matter your outside stress, you left all that garbage at the door. The next case was *that* kid's *only* case, their whole life possibly, and they deserved someone to look out for them, their "best interests," as the law would say. That was how Oskie navigated the ups and downs, the joys and hurts, the empathy for each kid who came and went through court, the same way Hollis had survived his twenty-five years on the bench.

Oskie flipped through the day's docket, skimming his notes on each of the names, but his mind drifted as he spread open the limerick book on the armrest of the couch.

[Journal Page 27]

One life you share with others, the other inside your head. You can close your eyes to risk, your heart cold and safe instead,

But that's not a cheat code to win life's game. It's a virus eating your mind's mainframe,

Makes you believe you're winning; you're really just playing dead.

Oskie winced and slapped the book closed after that one. He already knew the angles of his own heart. He could hear the angry voice in his mind telling Hollis, "I'm not ignorant. I *got* it. *All* of it. The last thing I need is you to lecture me, even from the afterlife." Oskie instantly felt regression to childhood, the aggravation teens feel when they are right, they know it, and no adult has anything more to offer them. But like many teens, his problem wasn't ignorance.

They are smart, informed, and they know what they know. The issue is the other hindrance to human progress—one not confined to teens but is instead a human condition—arrogance. Yes, people know what they know, but they refuse to accept that they don't know what they don't. And their resistance to the truth so often proves the very premise they deny. As Hollis would say in team meetings, "Some of you think I don't know what I'm talking about, and that's ignorance, but some of you think I'm not talking to you. You don't need this lesson. That's arrogance. And that's worse."

For Oskie, the lesson was simple. Empathy proved painful, often appeared unproductive and even at times useless. So what's the point? It's easier to detach, sure be a "good guy," and go through the motions but keep your heart insulated and out of reach. But that was his intelligence gaming himself, feeding his disdain, and intentionally denying himself the one thing he wanted the least but needed the most—social connection. Social connection is the one thing that heals pain and holds real purpose. Yet again, a man's arrogance inflates the bubble of his perception and walls off the cure to his own hopelessness. It's easy to dismiss empathy after you act in a manner that dooms it to failure. How could empathy ever really stand a chance alone anyway? Hollis would have thought the lesson equally simple, and both men would think themselves equally right.

"Judge Pete is inside, Oskie."

Ronny snuffed out Oskie's smoldering thoughts for a moment and reminded him that the nine a.m. docket call was near.

"Thank you, madam." Oskie paused as he opened the side door to the courtroom. "Hey … you doing okay? Anything you need from me?"

Ronny had long processed Oskie's need for purpose, for connection, and she didn't have to be a mother to read the fine print within Oskie's questions.

"Young man, you can always mow my grass or carry my groceries, and I'd be fine with a dinner date sometime, or even a double date, lest you think I'm too old for you."

A woman with Ronny's wisdom knew the man with the lost look on his face needed to feel useful to her, to the world somehow, and she would do anything to help him. She had given three options.

"Just text me when on the first two. You *will* be an old lady if you wait for the third."

Ever stubborn, even while clever and cute, Oskie exited to court, knowing he had declined exactly the one she wanted most.

Ronny, as Hollis had before his death, refused to give up hope that Oskie would find *someone*, a romance to remind him how joyful life and love could be. Anyone could see the charm that would make him the most eligible bachelor in Wilmington, if he ever chose to put his personality on display. He was quick witted, kindhearted, and hardworking, with handsome features chiseled from his Swedish/Greek descent and a life of athletics and exercise addiction. But he never allowed himself to consider and admit such appeal, nor care for such social objectives. Nonsense. Oskie would help any kid, and he had his tight circle of family and friends—Turbo, D-Tay, the Bakers, and the kids on his teams—but to others he almost appeared aloof in social settings, even though he disliked no one. He was engaging and lovable when exposed, but again he just had never found an answer to "What's the point?"

"Hey there, Big O!"

Judge Peterson bellowed his customary welcome as Oskie entered. Peterson was loud, large, and cheerful, sounding like James Earl Jones and looking like a black, bald Santa Claus. Oskie bowed a respectful, smiling nod and took the usual seat on the front row of the jury box, waiting for the clerks, attorneys, and caseworkers of the day to roll in. The judge fingered for Oskie to approach the bench.

"Got a couple extra tickets to UK-U of L this weekend. You interested?" he whispered, knowing there would be jealousy in the gallery if that info went viral.

"That's number one versus number two, Your Honor. You serious?" Oskie's face perked up. Turbo would be thrilled.

"Ronny has them in her top drawer," Peterson disclosed. "The missus signed us up for her nephew's wedding, and that's just not a hill worth dying on." He sighed out of mirth, a man proudly knowing he was right but also smartly knowing his place. "Just grab them before you go."

Judge Peterson was also happy with himself, knowing Oskie would take an excited Turbo or just *maybe* take a lady friend. Either way, a win-win.

Like Ronny, Judge Pete had known and watched Oskie grow as a young pup, and he had proved a subtle segue for Oskie after taking over Hollis's empty post-retirement seat on the bench. As Hollis's high school classmate, lifelong friend, and even sometime coaching partner, Judge

Pete had a fatherly understanding of Oskie but was better positioned as a nonparent to remotely guide his now-dead friend's son. As any parent or long-tenured coach knows, sometimes kids just need to hear a different voice.

From his first day in the robe, Judge Pete had quickly recognized Oskie's battle with what he called "Shadow Syndrome," as the father-son twosome spent the last five years of Hollis's career, and the first five of Oskie's, together at work. It was unintentional yet inevitable that Hollis had beamed and bragged with every step after Oskie returned to town to take the juvenile court probation worker post. Hollis saw opportunity. He could show Oskie the ropes, extend his own legacy, and see Oskie serve the greater good the way he had intended, hoped, and taught.

But the very job that returned color and pep to Hollis in those later years was also the very job that left Oskie in limbo about his purpose. The work posed a purpose of public service, but was it *his*? This was *Hollis's* workspace, *Hollis's* friends, *Hollis's* mission: merging the law and helping kids. Wasn't Oskie supposed to surpass his father? Hadn't Hollis drilled into him that to simply follow others was to waste his greater talents and opportunity?

Judge Pete knew that until Oskie, like his father, solved the notion of his own purpose; he would languish, stagnate, or even spiral downward. Over many a late-night bourbon, Judge Pete and Hollis had addressed many of life's mysteries and conjured the following sequence of a man's demise: no defined purpose leads to no perceived impact. That lack of vision or significance leaves an undercurrent of wasted time and insincerity at the bottom of all you do. A man can push only so many rocks without seeing progress on the mountain before him. Eventually, the absence of purpose leads a man to fear being either irrelevant or exposed as a failure, and that fear leads to apathy at his uselessness, and then to hate himself, others, or even life. It takes time, but if a man misses purpose long enough, he'll get to outright misery.

"Oskie."

Judge Peterson still had his grin. He nodded Oskie toward the back of the courtroom with, "Speaking of those tickets ..."

Oskie whirled to see Elly Parker and her smiling eyes, and he found himself halfway to her before he wondered what she might want. He was still focused on her eyes. Hollis's limerick may have called Oskie "playing dead," but Elly's lovely face proved he most definitely wasn't fully dead, not yet.

"Whatcha need, Ms. Parker?" Oskie needed to be useful, and he would gladly start with the beautiful social worker in front of him.

"I just wanted you to know I was assigned to Christian's case. We picked him and his brothers up early this morning, and he's asked about seeing you and Coach D several times."

She could tell her words left him torn, pulled by both the reminder of Boo's trauma and his realization of how good she smelled. Oskie's mind was caught in the middle, even as it moved faster than it had all morning.

"How is Boo? When can we see him?"

Oskie sought the info, but he also wondered how often he had actually recognized another person's scent. And actually wanted to stay close enough to enjoy it. He kept those last questions to himself, of course. Helping Boo had value; getting goo-goo eyed over Elly didn't.

"He's in a temporary foster placement, Oskie. Pretty rough night, as you might imagine." She paused with compassion to let Oskie process. "Nothing you've not seen before. We just didn't have any relatives that could take all five kids. An aunt and uncle over in Skidaway took the youngest two, and the middle twins stayed with the aunt in Fairview, but she's already got three of her own in a two bedroom. That left Boo by himself with us. He's on the docket for next week, and without a relative placement, he's likely headed to the St. Vincent's Children's Home until we find a permanent foster home and work on terminating parental rights for adoption."

"Okay, Elly." Oskie massaged his temples, trying to tame his thoughts into a coherent sentence.

"Take my number," she said as she handed him her card. "My cell is on the back. Get with D and let me know when you can visit. I'll meet you whenever. Sooner the better for Christian."

"Will post you after court as soon as I find D-Tay. Grateful for you, Elly. Please know."

His eyes bounced away even before his feet turned back toward court as the docket was starting. He was back in his seat in the empty jury box, his foot patting anxiously. He wanted to get through the day and fill D-Tay in with the details. He wanted to get to Boo to assure him all would be okay. He wanted to remember whether he had ever felt anyone look directly at and actually see him like Elly just had. He peeked back at her to maybe feel it again, but the social worker on call overnight was also the one without any cases set for court the next day, and she was gone.

— 9 —

STARRY-EYED DREAMERS

"Ditters is a good boy, Mr. Pete."
So said Shelly Stewart, the mother of the day's first juvenile defendant from the seat she always took on the front pew after the bailiff called her case. Stacy Stewart, a.k.a. "Ditters," was coming in on the transport van from the juvenile detention center in nearby Beaufort. This was Ditters's eighteenth different arraignment, adding to the largest juvy jacket in the courthouse and by far the largest example of a failed system. Ditters personified Oskie's thoughts of his job as nothing more than a meaningless cog in an aimless, inconsequential assembly line of justice.

"He just gets caught up with the wrong crowd sometimes, Mr. Pete."

Her sincere belief in her explanation belied Ditters as the common denominator in crime that had started with petty thefts and forgeries but then evolved into destruction of property, cruelty to animals, aggravated assaults, and finally his current charge, arson. The Wilmington sheriff had arrested him last night after he set fire to the home of his ex-girlfriend. She and her parents had survived. The structure hadn't.

He had done it. Everyone knew he had. The system would afford him a public defender and the usual due process, but ol' Ditters had finally committed a felony worthy of prosecution as an adult. At seventeen, after already spending a year in juvy detention and two other six-month stints on probation with Oskie, Ditters had earned early graduation—in other words, certification to stand trial and face real time with the big boys in the state penitentiary. "It's not the time you do. It's who you do it with," went the quote Judge Pete frequently recalled from his early career as the town's only public defender, wherein he fielded many a jailhouse call from incarcerated clients desperate for freedom. Indeed young Ditters's life was about to change. Thus, Shelly's ironically comfortable first-name rapport with Judge Pete didn't bother those in the know on this case, because today, in an otherwise gray line of mediocrity, the cogs of the system like Oskie would have their revenge.

"You know we have really tried to help him, Shelly."

Judge Pete's long pause and quivering lip before speaking supplied emotion on behalf of the whole system. He didn't see the impending punishment as revenge but rather failure to save a wayward soul. No matter the "crowd" Ditters ran with and no matter the obvious lack of parental influence from Shelly, the system was in place to reel kids like Ditters in, but this one had gotten away. And like he had learned from Hollis's example and lectures, its failure in that regard was also his.

Oskie understood Judge Pete's position, even admired the emotional investment, just like with Hollis and the empathy, but Oskie couldn't see past the obvious circus covered in a courtroom, with Ditters as the mascot clown inviting everyone in, front and center. Granted, a performer with Ditters's rap sheet was an abnormal mockery of their efforts, but the futility Ditters symbolized still seemed all too customary. Emotion or hope in the face of such a stacked deck seemed misguided.

You stay up late, think of every option, use every resource available for *years*, and a life still gets wasted. A house still burns down. You could just as usefully attack a windmill with a toothbrush.

But Pete, like Hollis before him, seemed to gather himself with gratitude and work his way through the muck and disarray of Ditters and a dozen other cases. By midafternoon, yet another juvenile docket was in the books.

"Well done, young man."

Judge Pete toasted Oskie with coffee back in his office, a congratulatory benediction notwithstanding the questionable significance of their service. Even in the face of tragic movie reruns coming before him, spoiler alerts to juvenile behavior built on generations of recidivism from fathers and grandfathers, aunts and uncles, Judge Pete retained his inner Santa and his belief in the mission.

"If it was easy ..." He nodded as his voice was drowned in the gulp from his cup. "Let us always be thankful for job security, Oskie. It's good to be needed."

Oskie could almost hear Hollis's voice in Pete's words, but though he resembled Hollis by never turning down a free cup of coffee—ever—his inner Grinch still countered with, *What's the point?* It was a rigged game. The law was "best interests of the child," and that always led to returning the youngster home, reuniting the family, even though common sense told you the end result once you released the kid back into the wild. After all, even Judge Pete would relent when cutting the kids loose from probation or detention or foster care; at some point the state couldn't impose a parenting playbook on the people. There are always basic legal boundaries of neglect, abuse, and dependency, but if a man leaves his teenager home alone while he heads down to drink at the local pub or poker game and the kid gets into trouble, is he disqualified as a dad? Or if a man does six months in jail for liquidating some local weed, is he still not a father when he gets out? We're not talking father-of-the-year awards obviously, but the lines of basic fathering skills are nuanced, even as the biological bond of a father is clear. The law recognizes a child's basic need for his or her family, even as it is unable to define or enforce exactly what that need is. Bad parents are still free to be parents, and under what governmentally imposed moral code would they be "bad" anyway? All that law and freedom makes total sense in a vacuum, but when you turn a wayward kid over to a wayward parent, that kid's way generally leads back to the courthouse.

That was the system to which they were committed, if you asked Hollis or Pete. Condemned, if you asked Oskie. Boomers may not get Twitter or Instagram or Bitcoin, and they may move too slowly or cautiously for a world at warp speed, but they get the big picture of life that can come only from living it—patience, perseverance, priorities—how to move glaciers instead of gigabytes and how to sacrifice a smaller battle to win the larger war. These lessons are taught only by time, the one thing millennials and Generation Z kids can't make go any faster.

Yes, Pete could share Oskie's feelings of futility masquerading as a sarcastic celebration of Ditters graduating from a seemingly helpless juvenile court system. But he had seen enough not to suffer over it. Eventually with time, the right effort produced the right result. You hope to rehabilitate as you prepare to incarcerate, but either way the slow attrition of bad apples off the street ensures a community's stability. One kid saved or another one detained is still one less kid who drives drunk into an oncoming car, shoplifts a local grocer trying to make ends meet, bullies another kid at school, or otherwise disrupts the lives of people we count on, the ones just trying to live with dignity and happiness.

"Remember, we just can never let *them* outnumber *us*. Now go do something fun."

To Pete, courthouse worker bees like Oskie or Ronny or Elly were the pillars upholding humanity, not cogs or ghosts in a sputtering machine. Those devout servants, toiling mostly in anonymity, were features of the program, not bugs. To Oskie, though, the jury was still out. He was reluctant to strap on Pete's legal superhero cape just as he had struggled to accept Hollis's empathy theory as a secret code to success. He refused to blindly drink any cult's Kool-Aid, even from his dad, without dispatching what he desired as his own superpower—discernment.

Oskie didn't need to ponder his next steps or the automatic smile crossing his face. No discernment was required as he slid the Kentucky/Louisville tickets into his backpack, said his goodbyes, and exited for the day. Even without the gift, Oskie's deeper questions always subsided as he walked up Central Street from the courthouse toward Wilmington Middle School, the same feeling he used to get in reverse while walking to the courthouse after school as a kid. It was the feeling of anyone going from work to play, from responsibility to freedom. There were some days when Oskie might have headed to the school to monitor the performance of a kid on probation, but mostly his school trips were coaching related, not work related. Work, worry, and the weight of his unanswered questions all fell away. For that brief walk, he was twelve again. And this time, he had the tickets in his pocket to show Turbo.

As the middle school's head football coach, a high school assistant coach, the local juvenile court probation officer, and the guy who brought the travel baseball team into the gym at six a.m., Oskie enjoyed easy access to the school where he had grown up. But he'd had that well before acquiring those titles in the last ten years. A wave and nod to the principal, Mr. Morris, on the way in—and his picture in the trophy case as the school's all-time leading passer—had been his key to the kingdom since he graduated. It was just past two thirty p.m., the last period of the day, and he set up shop in his familiar chair in the hallway outside D-Tay's fifth-grade math class. Here he would regularly get to see Turbo's first smile after the closing school bell, much the same smile he had just sported leaving work. In this regard, even Oskie colored himself lucky and grateful.

"And that ... superheroes, is how you solve for x!"

D-Tay was still ardently hammering away at algebra late in the day, and while peering in at him through the door, Oskie brightened at such "old-school" antics by a true tactician. Coach D pulled out all the cool stops, running to each desk to answer a question, breaking any lull with the latest ten-year-old jokes (those he cleverly overheard and stored from the kids at recess), and even calling kids by superhero names to come to the board to solve a word problem—and thereby saving the world from a fictional disaster. Imagination, action, comedy. What kid wouldn't love such math?

D-Tay's power surged and not just because teachers must never drop their shoulders or pout if they intend to survive in front of a room full of kids. As a teacher, D had found his tribe, and you cannot underestimate such comfort as a prerequisite to be turned emotionally "on" all day, as long as it takes, whatever it takes. Oskie saw that recognizable comfort in D-Tay's face, comfort that enables energy, leaks laughter, and prompts passion; and he crinkled his nose a bit with a sigh. He pulled out the limerick book to pass the time, and he imagined it would be nice to be that sturdy going to work each day. Hollis agreed.

[Journal Page 31]

We question life from time to time, and without answers we get doubt.
We lose grip on the daily climb, even think of throwing the bout.

Is our work all a waste?
Is life on nothing based?

Finding your place makes life sublime; can't quit before you see your route.

"Ten-minute warning! Let's go!"

D-Tay clapped encouragement as the school day dwindled. D made everything a game, just like he and Oskie would do at any practice. Kids aren't unique. Games, competitions, challenges are just more fun at any age. Coaches generally like teaching due to the similarities in motivating students in a classroom and players on a court. At a public school, you usually find a coach teaching math, drawn to the practice repetitions and the logic of making the right chess-like move to always get the right result. Coaches like absolutes.

You invest industriousness with more sweat and careful planning than the other guy, and you should win. That's why fewer coaches seem drawn to teaching an English or literature class. There are just far too many word choices, meanings, and interpretations in there. The stereotype is that coaches read or write less fluently or that they shy away from emotion, but it is more the absence of certainty that drives them away. If not math, look for a coach in social studies with affection for storytelling and the motivations of human behavior and physical education, no explanation required.

"All right, my people, start getting your stuff together." D-Tay held the classroom reins even as the murmurs grew with the bell coming soon. "Last play coming."

Math lent itself to coaches through demonstration and imitation too. All good coaches are thieves. You take a good play you see, shine it up with a twist, and use it as your own. Then you demonstrate to your players and ask them to repeat it. Imitation going in, imitation going out. With legs crossed and propped on his desk from the back of the room, D-Tay watched a young girl go to the problem on the chalkboard and ace the answer as time expired; that was as close as D-Tay could get to teaching a play all week and watching the troops score with it on a Friday night. He wouldn't care if the girl spiked the chalk on the way out.

Brrrring!

The hallway flooded with a pungent army of piranha, each child hungry, hurried, and most of all, happy. Turbo was no different. He pushed his way straight to Oskie with a smile, grabbed a hug, and dropped his backpack.

"I'm gonna walk with DA to his locker, and he wants to come over, okay?"

Turbo knew the answer, so it was more a notification than a request. DA was the travel team's second baseman and most likely to ask one hundred questions a practice and cross-examine an umpire, thereby earning his nickname.

"Of course, sir." Oskie nodded at DA too. "Fine on both counts. Double-back to me here. I need to talk to D."

Oskie watched the two boys march off arm in arm and let an

involuntary laugh escape. No matter the subject taught, another magnet for coaches who teach is middle school. Kids aged ten to thirteen are the perfectly situated underdogs, the most malleable yet least desirable in the school. Too old to be cute, too young to be cool. Old enough to want to save the world, young enough to believe they can. Still with so much to learn and still without the attitude that would prevent it. They are messy but also magical. Every coach is a sucker for such starry-eyed dreamers, including Oskie watching Turbo and DA saunter down the hall.

The crowd was clearing by the time D-Tay was closing up the classroom. He locked his door and turned with a wink and smile to Oskie, both men still temporarily distracted from the discussion of the day. Boo. His front-row seat next to Turbo had been empty all day, and no math lesson or memorable limerick could supplant that as job one.

"You got a plan yet?" D-Tay had presumed their partnership correctly. And Oskie had never let him down.

"Elly just texted a bit ago," Oskie reported. "We are set for tomorrow, and I've already taken the day off. Pick you up at eight?"

"How about seven? It's about a ninety-minute drive, right? I have to actually get back and at least work half a day, or else I can't coach tomorrow night."

D-Tay was also an assistant coach for the high school basketball team, and a February Tuesday always meant the district and/or regional tournament, if they were any good, and they usually were.

"That shouldn't be"—Oskie started but then stroked his chin in contemplation as he saw Turbo and DA turn the corner, coming back to them—"a problem ... except for Turbo. Hmm."

Oskie reverted to discernment mode. How much should Turbo hear or know? Should he even go? "Don't worry. I'll figure it out tonight. But might be three of us going. Bring your smile." Oskie grinned for good measure. The boys were fast approaching.

"Oh! I will, sir! Elly, eh?"

D-Tay grinned back with a face that feigned a thousand thoughts. "Shhhh ... shush!"

Oskie meant it. But his grin was genuine and still there.

— 10 —

GUILT IN OVERDRIVE

"Thanks for driving, man."

D-Tay was somber, without the spark of his usual "Hey now." His thank-you offered the lesser seen form of gratitude laced with sincerity. It wasn't the rote, mandatory repetition of a two-word acknowledgment a mother forced on her five year old in public places. Between real friends or in this case brothers, the words always passed over the specific detail of the day and pointed more to the overarching connection, as in, "Thank you for sharing life's burden with me." Otherwise, such words about the simple use of the other's car were tacit and unnecessary.

"No Turbo, eh?"

He actually craned his neck to the truck's back seat as if Turbo would be hiding in the floorboard.

"Nah. Felt a little heavy for him." Oskie's voice still said indecision. "Maybe I was wrong not to trust him with the truth?"

D-Tay let that thought linger in the truck, hopping out in silence for coffee as Oskie had pulled in for gas at the convenience store on the way out of Wilmington. Oskie blew into his hands for warmth by the pump, weighing the parental dilemma between protection and permissiveness. No parent ever always picks right between shielding children from hurt and letting them learn through pain. Perhaps some at least avoid overthinking the dilemma as an extremist. One side vows to let a child be "raised by wolves" and the stinging lessons provided by the natural consequences of their actions. The other side painstakingly intervenes as the bulldozer or helicopter parent, obliterating the problem or carrying the child away from it.

Oskie lay conflicted in the middle on telling Turbo about Boo's circumstances. Trying to balance Turbo's age, maturity, the seriousness, the necessity, the timing, and the uncertainty of the details, Oskie had opted for the parental fallback, a hopefully harmless half-truth. Parents habitualize the artful dodge, starting with Santa Claus and the Tooth Fairy. With Santa, for example, they rationalize that people are indeed rewarded for good, so it's a lesson taught, and someone does give love and gifts at year's end, so it's not a full lie, just not a magical guy in a red suit traveling the world by flying a sleigh overnight.

"Told Turbo that Boo was visiting family out of town a few days. I guess if you count our visit, there's a little truth in there somewhere."

Oskie sarcastically laughed off the indecision for the moment, remembering Hollis's inconsistent weighing of such concerns with him as a boy, and Hollis made decisions for others for a living.

In parenting, coaching, politics, or anything, when the path is uncertain, even the best of us find comfort by staying in the center lane.

"Luckily," Oskie continued as they pulled out on the highway, "Aunt Linda offered to drive Turbo to school and take care of CP later. If not, I might have had more 'splaining to do." Oskie had offered a Ricky Ricardo *I Love Lucy* accent to lighten the mood a bit.

"How was *your girl* this morning?"

D-Tay's responsive ribbing about Elly came across as contrived, as if he had known from the end of Oskie's last sentence that it was his turn to talk. Still, any words beat down the somber silence. And thus began the small talk to postpone the pending events of the day. Oskie had been to many children's homes, where ironically children were in process of separation from their homes. Oskie had already gone through that aha moment when he realized where all those vanishing kids in middle and high school went. Not the pleasant or humorous "aha" when you discover the feelings and fun behind the X-rated material you had read on a bathroom stall or had pretended to understand during a moment of braggadocio during a locker-room tale. This was the realization about the kids that became empty chairs, just like Boo's yesterday, ones typically near the bottom of the food chain in money, family support, and hope. Those kids didn't move to Beverly Hills with the Fresh Prince; nor did they find themselves magically in a movie, living a better life around the world. They generally went to detention for misbehavior—or worse, to some type of orphanage due to neglect or abuse.

Oskie had toured several jails too, either tagging along with his dad as a kid or when processing juvenile criminals now. When one steps into a jail, the instant impression is a wasted life. These are humans who had a chance and are squandering it. But an orphanage raises more ire inside you. You wonder why these kids never had a chance to blow. The jailbirds at least had some choice and maybe made at least some decision to fix their fate. But the kids in a children's home were not Ditters. They had earned their enrollment to state-sponsored misery only by the random misfortune of the home to which they were born, a home without protection, nutrition, or direction altogether. Moments inside such a place make your pretense of coaching and caring seem small and your home of puppies and PlayStation seem spoiled. Oskie had witnessed this story of Hollis's life from the front row. Hollis had turned that emotional experience into his personal mission and life's work, and though Oskie's mind questioned the impact of Hollis's efforts, his heart undoubtedly agreed with the need.

"You're awfully quiet, my man," Oskie offered. "You know he's going to be okay, right?"

Oskie thoughts had wandered through institutions before returning to the sudden awareness that his disconcerted best friend had grown up in one.

"Stayed up late thinking 'bout you. Tried to find you one that fit. I earmarked it and thought you might laugh. Check it out." Oskie nodded to the limerick book shoved between the driver's seat and console.

[Journal Page 35]

You wake to a life of lemons somedays, like the jerk in traffic cutting you off,
Always be thankful you notice their ways, ensures you have no flu, only a cough.

Bad times, bad people, bad things should pass
Every ignorant, arrogant ass.

But if your sense of bullshit goes astray, you've become a pig like them at the trough.

D-Tay read it quietly and then flipped through a few other pages before slapping it shut; not the laugh for which Oskie had hoped. D inhaled more than once to speak but aborted, and several minutes passed before he let it out.

"Honestly, Oskie, I feel like complete trash right now, as if I have spit on everything I tried to be about. I think Hollis would be ashamed of me."

His voice cracked. For all Oskie may have witnessed and understood, D-Tay was the only one in the car who had lived it. The closer the two got to Boo, the closer D-Tay's past crept in.

"Nonsense, D."

Oskie instinctively jumped to fix his friend but then paused. He had learned the hard way from his juvenile clients in distress and from raising Turbo that you must let people feel. It's messy and painful to watch, but you never validate others' emotions by running over them, even if you are just rushing to help them. A "fixer" or an empath, as Hollis had trained Oskie to be, must stay mindful to calm the hell down sometimes, even scream it inside his or her head if necessary. Odd that empathy would require a reminder to self that "it's not about me!" But even the most well-intentioned souls are arrogant, thinking they can fix everything. It's not about the fixer's need to fix; it's about the hurting's need to heal. Healing takes time, and the temporary mess, hurt, and tears during that process are necessary and should be left alone. The best thing a friend can be is present and patient, and often silence is the best response.

"Seriously, man." Oskie vowed to be silent after this. "You have to know you didn't cause this."

But D-Tay's mind was already spinning, and the caffeine and long ride finally overcame his suppression. His mouth began to speak his guilt in overdrive.

"After all I've been given, Oskie, I've become soft. How could I miss this and let it happen?"

Oskie knew D's thoughts and the weight of Hollis's familiar sermon, from which they came—well-intentioned teaching from a coach to his players to go forth and be productive, to pay your blessings forward. That was your duty, and the more you have, the more you must do.

"Hollis picked me up every … single … day. Hell, I stayed at your house five days a week. Your mom washed my clothes and fed my brothers and sisters for years.

"He never asked if I wanted fancy bats and shoes like the other guys. He always asked if I wanted to come over and hang out. We'd play cards in the dugout. Or chess, waiting for the next game. I know you know all of this, Oskie. Just saying that he knew what I needed. What really helped. And like you, he never let me down."

D-Tay's tension mounted; like an overwhelmed swimmer fighting the waves harder, his added panic just accelerated the drowning. Oskie remembered all of it, most of all how much D-Tay loved pleasing Hollis, the emotional connection with a father figure he had nowhere else. An "Attaboy, D!" from Hollis was the only time he had really smiled, and his smiling face lit up centerfield far more than his circus catches.

"Did you know I only saw Hollis cry three times? The two funerals and when he had to sign the order in juvenile court, sending me away. I know he had to. I knew it that day at thirteen, standing there, crying right back at him. But it killed him. So you know what he did? That joker bought me a flip phone and texted me every day for four years. Every day I was in placement until I graduated. He knew I lost everything." D-Tay paused for a sniffle. "But he never lost me."

The daily texts were actually news to Oskie, but he wasn't the least bit surprised. From the age of twelve, he still painfully well recalled a crushed Hollis telling the team their friend wouldn't be back, a memory partly preventing Oskie from telling Turbo about Boo now. Oskie's mind could still paint the toll shown on Hollis's face, reinforced when Hollis stepped back from coaching after that season. The team hung on one more year and then disbanded. Though it was nothing near the pain of D-Tay, the change had hurt Oskie and the other kids too.

Oskie took a place in the parking lot at St. Vincent's Children's Home just as silence took over their thoughts. Their past was no longer creeping on them but had now fully joined them in the back seat, gazing up with them at the cold, stone-walled, electronically sealed fortress holding Boo inside.

"Good timing, fellas."

Elly stamped her feet in the cold, waiting by the front door. "I already got him signed out of one class. You should get an hour with Boo before they do counseling and lunch."

"Just show me where."

D-Tay hugged Elly, his former high school classmate too, without much thought of her at that moment aside from thanks. He had a mission. Oskie nodded a thank-you toward Elly, a bit uncomfortable in her presence and thankful D-Tay's focus didn't notice. She led them to a conference room, walking by a window exposing a group of teachers' aides and caseworkers smoking in the courtyard. Nothing wrong with a smoke break, and likely all were caring, even heroic people dedicated to kids, but Oskie noticed, and D-Tay remembered the kind of person attracted to a job paying eighteen thousand dollars per year. Those workers deserved better, and kids like Boo definitely deserved better. They should pay star athlete money for the important work being done here. But forgotten kids somehow don't attract the money or glamor. Despite their comparative innocence, the kids in distress at decaying facilities fall behind prison reform to most politicians and voters. Maybe mistreated children are just too sad, so we look away.

"I'm okay."

Boo barely said much beyond that repeated phrase to all of the natural questions spewing from D and Oskie. It was as if the child were consoling the adults. That's what kids instinctively do when they see duress, even on those who should be protecting them. They grow up fast. They become the fixer. That's why neglected and abused kids still cried in juvenile court, missing the very abusive and neglectful parents that got them there. That's their parents and their life, and they instinctively love it. They cling to it. They don't know any better and don't want to.

"What are our options, Elly?"

D-Tay's inner teacher kicked in, and he wanted more for Boo than interrogation in a stale, musty isolation room. Boo had done nothing wrong, and he should feel that.

Elly poked her head out in the hallway and yelled at the desk clerk. She reentered with a smile and a "C'mon. Follow me."

She escorted the group and deposited D-Tay and Boo at the gym at the end of the hall. Really an old cafeteria with a cracked, slippery tile floor and a basketball goal at one end, but it was momentarily heaven. Boo ran ahead once he realized the destination, and D-Tay joined him for a few baskets and jokes. Fun and a few laughs were the perfect prescription.

Also perfect were Elly's style, her hair, her makeup, her jeans, and her cowl-neck pullover sweater, both what she had selected and how it fit her. Nothing was lost on Oskie, notwithstanding his awkward smile and nervously folded arms while waiting for D-Tay and Boo. He watched her walk the hallway, busy with another child, grateful both for the view and yet also her distance, which calmed his nerves.

Much like any gym in all the world, time moves faster for a kid there than in a classroom, and in a blink it seemed it was time to go. A little gym sweat turned back everyone's sadness for a bit, even as they had to say goodbye. D-Tay and Oskie exchanged hugs with Boo, exchanged dates with Elly for another visit next week, and then exchanged the cold of the facility for the cold outside. They tried not to look back as Boo and Elly disappeared, their smiles subsided and silence resumed, other than D's effort to steady himself with words.

"He seems okay, I think."

But once in the truck, D-Tay's veneer came crashing down under an avalanche of emotion built since graduating and being set free from St. Vincent's almost twenty years ago. His fists clenched, and he repeatedly beat the air above the dashboard in a silent scream. If there were words, they would have said to Hollis, *I'm sorry! I'm sorry. Please know I'm sorry. I should have saved Boo from this. But I will fix it. He will not stay here in this pain. He will not be me. No fucking way.*

Oskie waited until D-Tay had punched himself out, then started the truck. "I know, D. Promise, I know."

— II —

"Because They're Free"

The comrades that were Oskie and D-Tay became just two men in a truck going home, each lost in the distance of his own thoughts. D fought to clear his eyes this time, bobbing between accepting Boo's reality and the anguish of questioning why it had to be so. Oskie drifted between anxiety, trying to pick the right words to help his friend deal with the things to come and apathy, a part of him prepped for the possibility that Boo could be gone for good. Typical men, both torn by similar events and emotions just two feet apart, yet they were unable or unwilling to share any of it.

Oskie had taken the full day off and would mill around town while collecting his thoughts until lassoing Turbo after school. D-Tay had to find his center faster, still needing to teach the last three classes of the day and gather himself to coach in the district tournament that evening.

"You remember what you told me at my mom's funeral?" Oskie stated his thought aloud, not quite knowing its destination. He felt the instinct to help, to coach, but was tiptoeing between being too heavy or too trite. It was difficult to penetrate the mind of a friend so close he knew Oskie's thoughts before he thought them.

"You once quoted Hollis to me. 'Why you gotta make your foul shots? Because they're *free!*'"

The memory of Hollis's voice saying those words broke D-Tay's mental trance just as the truck pulled up at the front of the school to let him out.

"Seriously, man," Oskie said, trying further, "just like you told me at the cemetery that day, to use Mom's death as a reminder to not miss the easy loved ones around me—the foul shots and layups of life—to share and enjoy the ones closest to us every day. That's *exactly* what you said."

"That's what helped me take the courthouse job and reconnect with my dad. That's what spurred me to adopt Turbo. And I know you know all this, okay? But I can't *not* say it. Just too much Hollis in me."

Oskie was loquacious for once, so that self-deprecating observation brought more laughter than his actual words. He had his opening and needed to finish the thought.

"You've lost nothing D. It's all right in front of you. You'll support Boo through this. Whatever it takes. You made it, and he will too. But don't miss the foul shots to come thinking about the past missed shots, okay? Just like you told me, you've got kids to teach, to coach, a big game tonight, Mary Beth when you get home. All yours. All free."

D-Tay's eyes balanced for the first time since leaving St. Vincent's. Holding a perfect mix of tears from sadness and laughter, he did what men rarely do. He turned directly to Oskie with his heart and with the intent to give it.

"You're a good man, sir, and I love you."

When a man is wholly certain of what is real and true, few words are needed. D-Tay followed with a fist bump and went back to battle, knowing Oskie would do the same.

D-Tay indeed rejoined the fray of fifth-graders. Duty called. Oskie, on the other hand, had a fortunate few hours to regroup, and he let his mind set down the baggage of the morning while taking CP for a long walk around the streets of Whitemarsh. Oskie snickered as the pup pranced without a care in the world, outwardly boasting in spirit to any dog that might see his grand parade at two in the afternoon. Like most dogs, this mini schnauzer offered extreme energy and loyalty with minimal memory, and Oskie surmised that as the proper description of a best friend.

"I'm in town for the game. How 'bout we tailgate? I've got eats!"

Oskie fielded that text preview on his phone as he put CP's leash away, laughing aloud at the realization that his new adjectives for doggy best friend may also match his sister, Belle.

"Come on, Booas! Answer me. Six o'clock? Usual spot?"

Typical Belle. Maybe Oskie would have to add *impatient* to the definition. He didn't need to think long on the offer.

"I'm in, Booas [with added pig emoji]."

Oskie's usual succinct reply said all that was needed. He wanted to see her. He still felt their connection, reflected in the "Booas" nonsensical nickname they had called each other since childhood, and he was hungry.

If anything was omitted from the text, it was the energy Oskie needed from his little sis that day, the exact level of energy she always supplied. Belle was five years younger, acted five years older, and usually appeared five times happier. She had the kind of happy that comes from inner peace in motion, knowing exactly who you are and what you want and need and then creating your own comfort as the shepherd of your world, not as a sheep in the flock.

In her own way, Belle had also mastered discernment, but she opted for more optimism in the outcomes of her decisions than Oskie. Perhaps her power was circular. She was more decisive and thereby had more excess memory remaining in her brain's computer not having to overthink the decisions of the day. Picture two parts of the same tree trunk, both kids starting with the same hard drive, but both clearly branching apart with their own apps and designs as they grew older. Belle collected info, processed, and spit out foolproof plans. Hollis had failed to nickname her with any words shorter or sweeter than Belle, but as a child of the seventies, he might have tabbed her "Weeble," since "Weebles wobble but they don't fall down," and Belle was likewise a toy full of joy and balance, as if always right where she expected to be. Even on her missteps, the usual trappings of teenage mischief, she maintained her grace under duress. There was no memory of her ever getting caught at anything, ever.

Still, while their minds tracked apart, the base of their hearts remained tightly adjoined, each still fortunate to graft off the other whenever together. Belle had long tagged along with her big brother in bleachers, dugouts, and sidelines of games, ever excited to get a hug from Oskie or Hollis and to carry water to the boys. Sure, she liked the front-row importance and connection coveted by her classmates, particularly from kindergarten through middle school, and she played enough sports herself to appreciate the inner sanctum of the games, her brother's success notwithstanding. But Belle wouldn't have cared if Hollis and Oskie were playing checkers in the living room. The fanfare failed to make her radar; rather, her genuine affection for the two favorite men in her life was what drew her in. It was their time that thrilled her, and if a football field was where they were, then that's where she'd be. She just knew what was important and what wasn't, and such an emotional compass kept one clear and consistent.

Oskie could soak up solid footing from her clarity, though he didn't always take advantage of her gifts. She was a rock, full of love and adoration, always there, always thoughtful to his needs, always trying to earn his smile. But though successful somedays, Oskie usually discarded her affection as over the top, misguided family loyalty, the same as when Hollis bragged on him either as a coach or at work. Oskie's wiring worried of a catch to her gifts, thinking it undeserved. He had missed her full measure while growing up, misunderstanding that she didn't love her brother for his talents or skills or popularity. She reached for him because he was hers. And the only one she would ever have.

And that's why she smiled heartily as Oskie walked into the Wilmington High School music room just shy of six o'clock.

"Have you missed me?"

He offered his two pinching fingers and a sarcastic "Little bit," the only two words he could get out before giggling.

They were nearing three weeks since they had last met at Hollis's funeral, long enough to miss each other and long enough to misplace their sadness of saying goodbye to their father. Monthly visits were par for the course for them now, since Belle's life had sped up quickly and on purpose. While Oskie had meandered his way back to Wilmington, Belle had married her high school—and actually fourth-grade—sweetheart. Yes, she knew that soon. She had graduated from high school a year early by going to summer school and stiff-arming the social scene so many teen girls clung to.

Belle had no time for drama, even by the age of twelve. From there, she had beelined to a degree and career as an OB/GYN nurse at the local Lonesome Pine Hospital. No doubting, just doing. Top of her college class, happily married for a decade, and already advancing through their starter home into their hopefully forever home just across the county line in Nassau. She had added an adorable four-year-old son, Oscar, named for his uncle, of course; and if she had her way, a daughter was to come, spaced at just the same age as her and her brother. She lacked fairy tale or American Dream status only in that she worked too hard for a fairy tale, and her focus was too real for a dream. She earned the string of endless smiles the universe sent her.

"And I know you've missed this!" Belle smiled, pulling back the cloth on a basket of their favorite, tomato soup and grilled cheese, cut in kiddie squares for perfect dipping. This meal in the music room had been their secret hideaway and pregame ritual on Oskie's high school football Fridays. With the marching band on its way to the field to prepare for the evening's halftime show and other players occupied by goody bags and Post-it notes on their lockers from the cheerleaders and pep club, Oskie polished off soup and sandwiches with his sister. No performance, no pressure, just a vacuum of space and stress release.

And like old times, just with the music room vacated by a pep band heading to the gym for a basketball game instead, Belle and Oskie shared a pregame hour in their private space. Spacious, sound proof, and with ample avenues of expression, the room let Belle leave graffiti or art on the dry erase boards and allowed Oskie to dabble with his self-taught piano skills. The pair topped their play land with their "go-to" comfort meal, stirring memories of sledding and snowmen and snow angels during the winters of their youth, the shortness of breath and frostbite warmed only by their mother's soup or by a sister's replica of it now.

Oskie pecked out the tune of Deep Purple's "Smoke on the Water" as his unspoken thank-you, and Belle soaked up every note before they shared and devoured every last bite. Whether nonsensical jokes or satire on current events, their old habits returned, leaving Oskie relaxed enough to interject the news of his newly discovered limerick book, even at the risk of mellowing the merriment.

"Really! A whole book of them, eh?"

True to form, Belle seemed to take the news in stride, if not suspiciously unsurprised, like a kid who had already shaken her Christmas present but was trying to hide her discovery from the grown-ups.

"Where's Turbo tonight?"

She pivoted nervously from the limericks to the kids while inadvertently redirecting Oskie from his evening's pleasure to its pain. The kid rundown was uneventful. Little Oscar had stayed with Belle's hubby, and Turbo had spent the afternoon at the Boys & Girls Club before meeting them at the game. But in the fine print of those headlines was the realization of the game now nearing tipoff and their hour of peace in the music room done.

"Guess it's time to walk over."

And just that quickly, Oskie put his mask back on. Their peaceful haven gave way to the packed gymnasium, every face there for a different reason yet all a unified reminder to Oskie of why he avoided such events. His breathing grew deep and deliberate, noticeable to Belle, and she led him to upper seating by the wall, where he could recoil from the crowd. There was a rush of social anxiety, almost claustrophobic; only his gift of outer poise could hide his inner agitation. He supremely wanted to stay with Belle and see D-Tay coach, but his emotion had already predicted the outcome of the evening, in this case negative, and as in all cases exaggerated or wrong. That's what emotion does; it writes checks that reality fails to cover.

"There's your boys!" Belle intervened to distract, pointing under the basket to D-Tay, who was watching the team go through warm-ups with ball boy Turbo right beside, arms folded in imitation of Coach D. Oskie managed a nod and a small smile, rocking to and fro with nerves.

She pressed her hand gently against his thigh, as if to whisper, *See. What's real. What matters. You are so loved.* Belle sought to inject her peace into him, fresh blood that might wash away his habitual thought processes. But she knew all too well that you can give love freely and easily; you just cannot guarantee its receipt. Real love *always* knows it can't wear another's shoes, but it can only hope to try them on for a while, in hopes the loved one at least accepts a respite from his or her pain. Belle also knew well the source of Oskie's resistance, that which offered the only explanation for his misplaced agitation among a sea of adoring fans. Oskie owned this place. His picture and records were still on the wall. There were kids and now kids of those kids who all lit up when he walked in. Everyone put at least one eye on the guy they considered a hero, a classmate, even a friend. Oskie wanted none of it.

"D-Tay, think they'll win?"

Belle tried again to disrupt his thoughts, lure out his mind for coaching, lure out his heart for a friend. But she could never change what Oskie was, a child of competition.

That's not a knock on Hollis or all the lessons he had sought to teach—and that can be taught—through competition. He meant well, and competition undoubtedly hones courage, demands commitment to a cause, and culls the most skilled and talented from the pack. But the constant comparison to others lacks a finish line or a true sense of victory. No different from the millennial struggle with social media. There is *always* another drill or game or championship or Facebook quote or Instagram selfie. You are expected to win more points, more trophies, more "likes" without end. No finish line. No breaks. And the day you falter, you're forgotten. Those same fans become haters. The champ wins, but the reward is just a treadmill, an endless, anxious, and ultimately meaningless grind. The post-workout protein shake is an eternal, internal fear of inadequacy mixed with the façade of false success. The eventual response to that realization is anger and self-imposed exile. A millennial raised on social media will close his or her accounts at that point, and Oskie, the sports legend, could now barely stand to attend a game.

Yes, Belle knew her brother, an innate link strengthened by years of devotion as fan and friend. But she also had the benefit of later insight passed to her from Hollis; a limerick lesson coming after Oskie had matriculated through competition overload and long before he had found the book in the attic. She didn't need to thumb through Hollis's book to know one by heart.

[Journal Page 39]

Just. Try.
Know. Why.

True.
You.

Will. Fly.

It was forever her favorite memory of Hollis and one she relived often. Hollis had trained her on this one as a teen, making her the first fortunate follower of his modified philosophy. After a lifetime on his own competition treadmill, a middle-aged Hollis had taught Belle that life's wins come not against others but from improving oneself. Love harder, learn and earn more, and be healthier than yesterday. The words spoke a story both standing together and alone, and she wore the motto engraved on her heart, her north star to equanimity. Do not give up. Try every day. Know your value. Find the purpose that leads to passion. Be honest. Be only yourself and no one else. Do those things, and you *will* succeed. It's a fact. And that *real* success provides joy.

Oskie had already launched into adulthood before Hollis boiled life down so simply for Belle. Hollis had hoped to write it on Oskie's heart someday too, to somehow balance the ledger of any negative deposits he had made on Oskie's soul before learning the truth. That job fell to her now whenever Oskie was ready to receive it. She knew that too.

— 12 —

CURSING FOR EFFECT

"Will ya looky there, Booas!"

Belle pointed Oskie to the floor as the horn sounded. And Oskie's eyes met Turbo, hugging D-Tay in celebration, both pointing and smiling back at him. Oskie's eyes softened, and Belle was most thankful—not so much for the win but for the happy visual well worth Oskie's attendance. Even Oskie couldn't find sarcasm at the sight of Turbo, no matter his desire to dismiss the event altogether. He left it at silence while waiting for the nearby crowd to clear—silence she interrupted.

"Does that make you wish you were down there coaching?"

His teeth poked lightly through window shades of his lips. No one could resist Turbo's joy, and he had to admit that—deeper thoughts aside—it was always better down on the sideline as opposed to sitting among the crowd. He ignored the fans shuffling to the exits and eyeballed the team and Turbo in the postgame processional shaking hands. Even Oskie would still admit the basic virtues of respectful competition.

"Y'all headed straight home?" Belle refused to give up on engaging him. His eyes never left the court.

"Yeah, it's been a long day, Belle."

His words were weary. He had started the day early with D-Tay and Boo, and now the last ninety minutes or so of emotional pain tolerance had finished him off.

"Hey, thank you so much for the soup. You're always sweet to me."

He glanced at her face to make sure she felt sincerity, not the polite cover she knew he showed everyone else.

The team and Turbo had made their way to center court for a last meeting before dispersing amid a sea of students, parents, and girlfriends. Oskie's eyes floated up and across the gym, where Elly's face and eyes made contact. Propped against the wall at the end of the top row, she was the only motionless vision in the view. She sneaked a furtive eyeful of Turbo dancing as the band played "Celebrate" by Kool & The Gang; then she glanced back with a grin at Oskie as if to shoot him some of that happy from across the room.

"What's Elly doing now?"

Belle's inquiry didn't miss a beat. She had followed his face and felt the bounce of his leg against hers in the cramped gymnasium seats.

"She's a social worker. She helped us see Boo today."

Oskie was explaining away anything Belle might think—standard procedure for him to mark off emotional distance. *Nothing to see here. Move along.* She nodded slowly, knowingly, both in what he was doing and that he was full of crap. She knew the story on Boo, but Elly's involvement was news.

"Time to collect the Turbo. Meet me by the backdoor, and we'll walk you out, okay?"

Maybe he was tired. Maybe the crowd had finally fizzled away. Maybe he knew his cover was blown. But it really was time to get home—a coincidental getaway from Belle's inquiring gaze.

Oskie skimmed across the top of the bleachers to meet D-Tay with the usual post-win pound hug. Coaches generally mill around after victories, pretending to clean up, count stats, or talk to the media, but mostly just not wanting to leave their wonderland. Just in stepping off the bleachers to floor level, Oskie was reminded of the different world that existed for those in the action—a surreal shift from his four quarters in the stands, where the vast majority had only passing interest and/ or knowledge of the event below. D-Tay and company had put months of blood, sweat, and tears into preparing for that tournament, while those in attendance just a few feet away from the game had put in about five bucks. Suffice it to say, the interest levels of the two factions varied proportionately. Oskie held those cards close to the vest, aware of preserving D-Tay's coaching buzz. Few highs match the complete immersion of a coach in his craft, and a big win erases all the side effects. No fatigue, no stress, no bitching about being underpaid. It's priceless. You'd do it for free.

"Nice job with the trap out of that last timeout, sir." Oskie eye-rolled his compliment at the oldest trick in the book.

"It worked, didn't it?"

D-Tay scoffed back playfully. Mary Beth had poked her head in under his arm. Turbo was already starting to sweat in the middle of a pickup game, using a crushed concession paper cup as a ball. Belle had her coat on by the door and still had a thirty-minute drive home. It was time to go, even for the earth's most talkative species known as coaches.

"Seriously, man, congrats on the win. You deserve it."

Oskie corralled Turbo, and they joined Belle on a silent walk toward her car by the music room. He welcomed the smack of chilly air across his face as good medicine after the heat and congestion of the game, grateful for the win as good medicine for D-Tay, who would sleep well now even after the tumultuous trip to Boo that morning. Belle welcomed her brother back, who visibly relinquished his tension each step farther away from the gym, and she thought gratefully about the moments Oskie had shared with D-Tay, good medicine to remember the fun of friends and coaching. Turbo welcomed thoughts of raiding the refrigerator when they got home, but he thought very little before falling asleep on the way.

Turbo cackled at the snow on the ground the next morning. Not enough to cancel school in Wilmington but enough for him and Oskie to pull on matching mittens and beanies. Even CP had a sweater on over his fur while he did his business. Just a pit stop in the yard while the truck warmed up, as temperatures under 20 degrees canceled any long walks for the pup.

"Mucho coated!"

Turbo screamed while kicking up some snow. He had beginning Spanish for his first class of the day, and that was the description matching his limited vocabulary and unlimited exuberance. A treat on the kitchen floor to get CP back inside, the zipping of backpacks as the truck doors slammed, and then Turbo's "mucho coated!" on repeat at various volumes. Those were the sounds on the five-minute ride to school.

"Nothing fancy going on today, sir. Meet you at the gym after school."

A light head butt of their beanies added a nonverbal "I love you," and Turbo hopped out, ready for action. Oskie watched him walk in, wondering whether the water in his eyes was from the cold weather or his warm heart. Two years into fatherhood and five years into coaching, Oskie was comfortable managing kid details, still not so much on kid emotions.

Wednesdays were late-work mornings for Oskie. No court activity, just processing paperwork and managing cases from his basement courthouse office. And though it wasn't on the agenda in the middle of February, Wednesday evenings were usually saved for the midweek travel team baseball practice. So after dropping Turbo at school, Oskie's Wednesdays routinely turned toward the Wilmington High football field for a workout. He had long given up analyzing his unwavering commitment to working out six, sometimes seven, days per week. But if he was honest with himself, he juggled his routine to include everyday exercise for three reasons.

The first was competition. The strongest addiction of your childhood doesn't dissipate on its own. You have to actively choke it out, or it will just shift shapes to survive. Oskie outwardly disdained the gym crowds and their mirrors, stringer tanks, and cell phones—all proof of pettiness. But within Oskie's mind, he welcomed all comers, and this was means to exact undeniable revenge on all of them. They may not even know of the challenge, but they couldn't prevent him from outworking them, from outperforming them, with every rep and set. Even Father Time could join the game, and Oskie would defiantly pretend that he wouldn't grow old, at least not yet. He was in better shape than most twenty-year-olds, but among forty-year-old government bureaucrats, he was a physical freak. He admitted the narcissism at play, but it was harmless, it was solitary, and it satisfied his need to compete.

The second was clarity. Something about the mindless counting of reps for an hour distracted the brain from its baggage. Oskie was always able to enter another world at the weight room door, just an objective to reach, a plan to get it done, and a stopwatch as a witness. In any gym anywhere, it reduced to wiping sweat, controlling breaths, and dividing numbers. If a set was divisible by four, he would analogize to quarters and use all the old psychological tricks he had acquired from sports. First rep got out to a lead quickly, second rep finished the half strong, third rep was most important to turn it on when others were tiring, and fourth rep was the downhill finish. If divisible by six, he had similar techniques for innings of a youth baseball game. If by ten, he would matriculate himself down a football field ten yards at a time. These were mind-numbing mental gymnastics to many, but they cleansed his mind. Blame the endorphins or the sense of achievement, but by the end, Oskie had earned superhero status. Write a sonnet, solve Einstein's equation, or save the world—he was optimistic, clear, and confident from his sweaty conquest. For an overthinker, the post-workout coffee was the best ten minutes of the day.

The third was connection. If Oskie could call Hollis on some magical phone line to the past, there were certain areas of life that were prone to dropped calls or worse, lacked any service at all. After leaving his Wilmington roots behind as a young man, Oskie had returned to the town, the courthouse, and the world of youth sports—so many things Hollis like—somewhat kicking and screaming. Depending on the day, Oskie's enthusiasm for those things varied from one bar of complete indifference to two or three bars of "I'm not convinced it's worthwhile, but it's the best of the known alternatives." He had cast his lot with fatherhood too, and his love for Turbo—like Hollis's love for him had been—was always at full strength, but even that cell tower wavered from Hollis on exactly what parental lessons he should impart. Still, the one phone line that never failed to connect the two was working out. It had always just been fun. And it still felt as close to his dad as he could get.

Three things, ready made for a coaching speech, all Cs for catchy alliteration and all crafted in the short truck ride to the field. Hollis would smile.

Entering the old Wilmington stadium always brought to mind other memories. Start with the tired concrete beneath the rusty gate with the creaky joints. Oskie had climbed this many a day in his youth, even covered in snow like today and even while toting a tire to pull by rope during sprints. Long before the day of fancy sleds, Hollis had made resistance running a staple of their training, complete with a tire and rope in the trunk. Just inside the fence were the signs recounting the results of each season. Perhaps the only item updated over the years—a line adding each team's record at the bottom—and perhaps the only tangible remnant of what occurred in those days long gone. The signs were symbolic of the very nature of the past, each year backward, colder, paler, and smaller as you go.

Oskie traced the narrow walkway onto the track and field, usually littered with pep club graffiti encouraging the players, and he recalled the clickety-clack of cleats that sounded the alarm for the game to come. It was silent and empty and white with snow, but Oskie could smell the Friday night grass in the fall, hear the scoreboard horn and silly public address announcer, and see the faces of friends in the huddles, each peeking at him through face masks for their marching orders.

But as he surveyed the turns of his first warmup lap around the field, he savored more than just sports. This field was often their family playground, perks of Hollis having a coach's key. There were many family fun days, just playing catch or chasing a Frisbee or flying kites. A toddler Belle could ride her tricycle, and a hyperactive puppy Mia could roam free to the point of exhaustion. Oskie reached the third turn of the track, remembered as his favorite assignment on the relay teams since it adjoined the school's tennis courts. He could count on lots of pretty female scenery on that end of the field.

Hitting the backstretch to the finish line, Oskie upped his pace.

Like the end of any lap of life, you shed fatigue and seek inspiration for another round. You are not the weaker shell of yourself the past proclaims you to be; you are just leaner from experience, more agile as you dispose of the waste from your life.

In fact, Hollis had just said it better that morning in the limerick Oskie had fast made a daily habit of reading.

[Journal Page 43]

Recognition and fame stay not the same; first they applaud you but soon become harsh.
Your victory comes in not playing their game; fake fans are plenty, and real friends are sparse.

Clean out your closet; take all to Goodwill.
Spit out their venom; it's a poison pill.

You need not defend yourself or explain; you'll never please them. To try is a farce.

Thoughts of those words while passing by the tunnel to the locker room ignited the fire of Oskie's favorite, and likely most impassioned, coaching sermon Hollis ever gave.

"I know you're disappointed, gentlemen. You know I am too."

Hollis began with an obvious understatement. This was his "corner cake" best team, now all grown up, a top-ten team statewide, with his son now the best quarterback in school history. And there they sat midseason at 3–3, two of those losses heartbreakers in overtime, struggling to figure out why. Meanwhile, as everyone in the room knew, Hollis and Oskie were still adjusting to Annie's death from the previous summer. That alone left the air in the room heavy as Hollis, who helped call the plays as an assistant in the press box but rarely addressed the team, began to speak.

"I know you think yourselves treated unfairly. That you deserve better."

Regardless of whom or what was to blame, unfortunate injuries, coaching mistakes, player complacency, the players were beleaguered less by their slow start, which could still be corrected, and more by their fans having turned to haters, which couldn't yet be understood. Call them thin-skinned teens, but they were stung by the speed and severity of the venom spit at them with each loss. The head coach knew Hollis's relationship with this particular set of seniors, and heading into the game of the year against archrival Fayetteville, they had agreed that pregame words from him could stand the best chance of righting the ship.

What the other coaches didn't know and what made the speech even more perfect to Oskie and the seniors closest to the family was that on top of losing Annie, Hollis was facing a stiff political challenge that fall, a candidate without concern for fair play. There were rumors spread of Hollis's misuse of the Boys & Girls Club for his own financial gain, all untrue, but the small-town mob smelled blood, and the feeding frenzy attracted many of Hollis's presumed friends. He was stinging too. It was a lot to carry all at once, and it hurt.

"I always emphasized to you empathy, to feel for others over yourselves."

To that point in his life, Oskie had always seen Hollis soldier on with a good face, but the boys were about to see his true heart.

"But the game has changed, men. They're not playing by the same rules."

Hollis meant social rules. Whether from ignorance, arrogance, jealousy, or just outright cruelty, the rule breakers appeared to outnumber and outflank the rule abiders, rendering the practice of Hollis's empathy religion impossible. Hollis often talked of getting off the sidewalk for someone, when it was too narrow for two people, or letting someone cut over in traffic. It was the courteous, polite, and "right" thing to do. But as he got himself lathered up, others realized he felt boxed in by a world that didn't reciprocate that kindness. When you're the only one perpetually giving way, you get nowhere; you even go backward, while the ignorant and arrogant seemed more blissful and blessed.

"I know I told you to keep your religion. That it's on 'them.'"

Hollis always gave the homeless guy on the corner a five-dollar, ten-dollar, or twenty-dollar bill, even knowing from the man's court file that he might easily smoke or drink it away. His approach would say, *Give it to him anyway. If he misuses it, that's his sin, not yours.* But he was now tired of seeing no fruits from his efforts … broken … angry. And Hollis had decided, since the joke was on him, and since his boys were learning the same lesson at the same time, why shouldn't they share the tragic laughter together?

"But I was wrong, men. It lies with you and me."

From there, he launched into an analogy no one on the team that night would forget. And it is still known as the "*Gladiator* speech." Hollis first described the plight of the hero in the movie *Gladiator*, a general turned to slave, his home and family destroyed brutally, forced to fight for his life to appease arrogant rulers and amuse a most-ignorant public. Surely no one could argue their plight was as bad as his.

"You have to make a stand. Let it all out! Right now!"

The movie hero did the only thing possible to sustain his manhood. He stood up for himself, used his anger against them and for himself, never mind the poor sheep in the way that might be slaughtered, whether the other slaves in the movie or the other team across the field that night.

"And when you're done tonight, you let them know it's not for them but for you! I want you to spit, slam your sword, look up in the crowd, and scream, 'Are you not *fucking* entertained?'"

Hollis added an expletive that night in his crescendo, one that would have ordinarily brought down the house in laughter. Hollis never swore much and had never grown comfortable or clever with it, so he seldom tried but for the "effect" of drawing a laugh to break the tension. But he was clearly fed up with that season, maybe with life in general, and by the end of this particular talk, he was every bit Russell Crowe or Denzel or Travolta, the coolest cat in the room. The team was already standing, clapping, marching, and screaming past him into the tunnel, even before he reached the end. The boys proceeded to whitewash an otherwise-equal opponent, 32–8, with Oskie throwing four touchdowns and Hollis feeling like every play he called couldn't miss.

— 13 —

WHAT'S THE POINT?

It was nearing ten a.m. before Oskie's post-workout glow subsided, his sigh sounding the reminder of the day's drudgery ahead. Mounds of case files and multiple computer screens, toiling while locked away in his small office in the basement of the courthouse. His one window faced the scenic brick wall of the county jail next door, and the ladies in the sheriff's office upstairs called it the dungeon for good reason. Oskie never shied from a hard day's work, but the non-courtroom days were the longest and least inspiring, and he would rely heavily on an endless stream of coffee.

It was a decent job as jobs go, and the dungeon days were a small price to pay for the perks—decent pay and benefits, setting your own schedule, the chance to clean the community of bad apples, or on the flipside, replanting a kid in a better life. But it was on these days, shared with the repeating rows of recidivist files, that Oskie felt any optimism a delusion, and he was convinced his work lacked any impact whatsoever. There was no *Gladiator* glory to exhort here, and even if so, much like Hollis's speech that night, an emphatic statement and big win are just great deodorant. The underlying, unresolved source of the smell still remains. Lipstick on a pig. That team with great expectations and talent, for example, still finished 7–6. All the kids with great expectations and talent, filling up his juvy casefiles, still returned to the courthouse.

Oskie sat down at his desk, split between feeling right and not wanting to be, and he imagined that Hollis had faced the same daily crossroad of concern. Helping others felt good.

Your emotions want empathy to be right. But is it not just daily suicide when the majority of society doesn't buy in with you? Just death by a thousand cuts?

Oskie could hear Judge Pete's voice imploring that we "can't let *them* outnumber *us*?" But what if that was already the case? How do you answer intellectually to the fact that kindness to the world is no longer cost effective? That most just selfishly take and abuse generosity, and suck it dry, even if just to waste it or for their own amusement? That the world proves Hollis's ignorance and arrogance as the ailment of mankind much more than his empathy as the antidote? That the average person is unaware of others' needs or just doesn't give a shit? If so, you can say your kindness is not weakness on your social media all day, but you're giving with no return on your investment, and that makes you a sucker. You're left with "What's the point?" Again.

"You got a minute?"

A knock and a voice at the door unknowingly caged Oskie's runaway mind and called to his heart. Though her face was partially obscured by the reeded glass windows, he knew the face of his visitor immediately and lost any thought he had just ten seconds ago. It was Elly.

"Hey there, Elly. What's going on?"

Oskie opened the door and held on to the knob for balance as her beauty breezed by him. She stepped inside and paused to look around. He was certain she had never been in his office and just as certain that they had never been together behind a closed door. He wouldn't have forgotten the electricity on his skin.

"Sorry if intruding, Oskie." She offered social graces, but it was unnecessary cover. Elly was the antonym of trepidation. She was instantly welcome anywhere, and she was still fingering the certificates and pictures on the bookshelf as she continued. "Judge Pete said you'd be down here … I wanted to catch you up on Boo while I had the chance."

There was a calm cleverness to her, almost coy, as if she knew something you didn't but had just decided not to use it right now. Elly's essence hinted at regality. You could picture her as queen of the earth but one who relinquished her crown, knowing she was needed in the trenches, a woman better suited not as a "princess" but as a steady, independent fixer of those around her, as a social worker, as a mother, as a woman. Take away the pretty, the soft yet muscular curves, the safe yet hypnotic eyes, the seasoned yet ageless skin, and you'd still be drawn to her, but she had Oskie's full attention on both counts.

"You're welcome to sit if you want, Elly." Oskie pointed her to a chair and headed for his. "I'm just moving cases today … nothing glamorous going on 'round here."

Oskie's words played his stock defense in the face of any bubbling emotion, leaving any direction up to them while downplaying his interest or value. His body portrayed a bit of offense though, albeit nervous at possibly taking a shot. He buttoned down the butterflies long enough to smile at Elly with his arms folded and eyes darting around the room.

"I figured you and D would both want to see Boo again," she started, "so I just need to pin down a good day. That's the easy part. What I hoped to get from you is a little inside information."

Elly paused a second, perhaps trying to read the racing thoughts behind Oskie's face. He was intent on every word, but each was also an excuse to study her face and mouth. Meanwhile, half his mind had regressed to high school, turning her words into the obvious puns, as in she could have *any* inside information she wanted.

High school might have explained his unusual aplomb allowing him to monitor the conversation and still muster the split-screen sexy thoughts in his head. No, they had never dated or even been close friends while growing up. They were three years apart, she a freshman and Oskie a senior; and beyond a couple of classes together, they'd had but few conversations. Still their lives were very much mirrors. They shared high school sports stardom, Elly being to Wilmington girls' basketball what Oskie had been to football, complete with the disillusionment afterward. They both struggled later to find footing amid trauma in their twenties, Oskie dealing with the deaths of Annie and Pookie, with Elly enduring an emotionally abusive marriage capped by her spouse's death roughly ten years in. And now they were separately settling into single parenthood, both with fifth-grade kids and connected careers in the courthouse. She was real to him, a person he knew closely despite distance, a story he heard without words. He appreciated her stamina and admired her courage, because he could literally see and feel every day of her life.

"I'm wondering if you would feel out D-Tay's intentions on Boo. I mean, I know he wants to help, but I need to know if he and his wife would seriously entertain taking him in."

The voice of her proposal recalled him, reversing his retrogression.

"The vibe I'm getting from Boo's next of kin is that he's a little more than they'd like to strap on," she posed, "*if* there's a definite better place for him. They understand Boo is very fond of D-Tay, and that D is a stand-up guy, so if he offered to take Boo, I think the aunt and uncle would agree to sign over temporary custody. Especially with Judge Pete around, that would put D in a great position to permanently adopt once we terminate parental rights.

"But if D's not interested, I expect they'll keep Boo as opposed to risking an open adoption process that could send him anywhere.

"The obvious upside is keeping Boo stable and close with his current friends, school, and support system. But the brothers, the aunt and uncle, the extended family—they would all need and want visitation. And at some point Boo may have to face his real mom and dad if they show up at the final hearing or even after termination of parental rights, especially if the dad stays local. Guess I'm saying D would be adopting the whole family situation, more than just a child. Sometimes that's too much for potential parents to chew.

"There is some financial help that comes with Boo at least, but that's also why I can't try to sway either side. If he wants Boo, you're in the best position to connect the dots."

Elly had effectively laid out Oskie's mission, succinct but with just a slice of sassy. That was her manner with everyone, a melody that had simultaneously sung Oskie's nerves to sleep. Realizing she had stopped talking and that it was his turn to speak, he noticed his shoes pushed against his desk drawers, coiling himself back in his chair, knees against his chest.

"I'll see D this afternoon. How 'bout we try this …"

Oskie had a question for D-Tay, but it was surrounded by questions for himself, questions that wanted to raise their hands and be called upon, but like the scared ten-year-old he suddenly felt like, they were afraid the audience may think them dumb. He opted for the easy road.

"Let's plan another visit to St. Vincent's this weekend, and that will give me a few days to *really* talk to him. Could you set us up for Saturday morning?"

The loudest questions left unsaid came from the Kentucky/Louisville basketball tickets screaming from inside his center desk drawer, Judge Pete's gifted great seats to number one versus number two, a game also set for that Saturday. The game was at three p.m., and St. Vincent's was halfway to the arena.

Could the St. Vincent visit be timed to go on to the game from there?

Should he take a chance on an actual date?

Would she say yes?

Oskie's right hand gestured slightly, wanting to spill, but his left hand moved to his mouth, clamping the leak. He looked at the drawer holding the tickets and actually felt his feet push it harder closed. The clamor of inner questions had been quelled by the risk-averse law of the land in his head. If in doubt, the answer was no. He could even cloak it in nobility, since this meeting wasn't a social call but about D-Tay and Boo, a much more important matter. And Elly was likely busy with her son on Saturday anyway. Fear always likes excuses, even when foolish; the more the better. Quantity over quality.

"Sounds like a plan then."

Elly took Oskie's pause as her cue and rose to leave.

"Post me when you know Saturday is a go, okay? And I'll text you back some options on what time we can meet." She smiled back at him as she reached for the door. "You've got my number."

Yes, he did. And she had his too. There was no doubt in his mind about that.

Oskie knew he had finished the workday because the computer files were all updated, and the paper files moved from his desk to the cabinet. He also knew he had glided up the street to pick up Turbo after school because he was standing in the high school hallway, watching basketball practice through the slim rectangular window in the gym door. He still did not know, despite multiple conversations with himself, whether he should ask Elly to the game on Saturday.

Oskie knew Turbo was happy, because he was a ten-year-old boy with a basketball on the side goal in the gym, a few feet from high school boys he admired and a few feet from high school girls, the warming-up cheerleaders waiting for practice to end, whom he admired for different reasons. Oskie also knew D-Tay was happy, because he was a coach energetically guiding the team through paces before delivering the closing sermon on the day after a big semifinal win and the day before the district championship game. He still didn't know, despite multiple conversations with himself, whether he was truly happy or whether he would ever be.

Oskie waited for eye contact and a wave in from D-Tay, who welcomed him without breaking coaching stride, before slipping into a corner seat on the bleachers. All coaches, best friends or not, knew not to disrupt the focus of a practice uninvited. Even Turbo knew to hold the ball and halt any noise whenever a drill stopped for a coach to speak. Oskie quietly settled in, observing the unusual level of energy over the last ten minutes of a practice. The kids could sense the climax of the season, a championship or bust, just twenty-four hours away. They would be the underdog against the newly consolidated Tybee County High School across town, but it would be late first quarter before talent, skill, team chemistry, and execution of the game plan would take hold. From now until then, players and coaches got a glimpse of invincibility, the feeling that anything was both possible and positive.

Oskie sardonically cycled through all the times he had built himself up for the next big game, the next season, the imagination of winning every game, regardless of how many times the usual results of your experience teach you the opposite. The religion of sports so often sold hope and faith unjustified by reason; the same was true for the religion of romance. There he sat, aglow at the precipice of a date with Elly, intrinsic biology and chemistry encouraging him to jump, while his statistical analysis of history proved otherwise. Was a date possible? Assuredly. Could it be a positive experience? Likely. Would the endeavor evince his present emotion later? Highly unlikely.

Still a quiet spectator at practice, Oskie doodled the comedy of his thoughts, Hollis style.

> [Oskie's Gym Note]
>
> Faith demands no memory.
> Hope wants you too blind to see.
>
> Let everything go.
> Forget what you know.
>
> Then relearn it … painfully.

— 14 —

THE THREE BONES

A resolute team chant concluded practice and commenced the coach's powwow. Players think coaches talk too much during huddles and team meetings, but those are minor league compared to coaches swapping stories and laughs afterward. Coaches' mouths are their last remaining athletic muscle, and since they will always crave competition, their objective becomes telling the funniest or most entertaining story, no matter how many times it's been repeated or how long it takes. Turbo was a quick study of the coaching species in his two years as Oskie's son. Turbo grabbed a quick hug from his father and ran as the pack of coaches took shape, their social formation confirming at least another hour of gym time. Somedays he would respond with a well-placed groan or innocent insult to his two favorite old men, but today Turbo consoled himself by letting the pretty cheerleaders pinch his cheeks.

Oskie would not try to win coaches' story time this particular day. He offered a few counterpunches of conversation for courtesy but mostly bobbed and weaved on the edges while waiting for the herd to thin out. He had a deeper discussion with D-Tay on his mind. The pals needed to cover the new ground on Boo and, after Oskie's thoughts had spiraled downward while sitting around, perhaps rehash more aged territory on life. Oskie knew the combined triggers creeping in on his psyche, the uncertain emotions on Elly today, and the most certain emotions of Annie's birthday tomorrow. It would mark the twenty-fifth year since his mother's death, and though Oskie refused to let any of his mourning ever metastasize to others, he also knew he needed a quick hand with the heaviness to keep from crashing. Like spotting lifts in a weight room, emotional spotting is an art among men. It must be just enough to complement strength yet not too much to connote weakness. It had to be a familiar friend, and for Oskie, that meant D.

"Honestly don't know how you do it, sir."

Oskie had long wondered the source of D-Tay's limitless zeal for coaching, a zest reinforced by what Oskie had just seen over the last thirty minutes. Today, though, as they nested near the scorer's table as the only two coaches left in the gym, Oskie's curiosity carried over to D-Tay's appetite for life as well.

Oskie understood that D-Tay got his coaching chops from Hollis, immersing himself in the flurry of Hollis's sayings and sermons, most of which D still used on his new generation of players. But it was more than just repeated rhetoric. Somehow Hollis's influence had infected his soul. Gone was the pained and stoic "you can't catch me" kid Hollis had found, morphed into the sweaty, satisfied man sitting there, flourishing in his perfect fit as a coach. So Oskie's question wasn't directed at how D had forged his path but more on how he kept his compass directed north and going forward.

"Championship tomorrow night, my man. Motivation is easy this time of year."

D-Tay shrugged off the question with the obvious, but he knew Oskie's voice meant more, and Oskie knew D-Tay knew it. D-Tay just wanted to push Oskie to ask more directly.

"Aren't you tired? Do you *ever* get tired, D?"

Oskie kept chipping away, still fighting internally against burdening his friend with emotional baggage. His intended questions were more about happiness than fatigue, as in "How do you stay so happy?" or in more cynical terms: "How do you stay so hypnotized?" "In the face of facts against you, evidence that all your teaching and leadership fail to protect kids from the fates, how do you dive in daily and give a damn anyway?"

"You know what makes me tick, Oskie. You really want me to spell it out for you again?"

D-Tay took the wheel and turned the talk more directly. "My passion is meeting needs," he explained, "finding or creating the family that I've lost over my life. Family isn't just biological. It's the people just like you … those who need you … your true peeps. It's you, it's Mary Beth, it's the kids I teach. I feel the gift of the help I give to them, and I can feel the gift of family in return. Fills holes both ways."

Oskie respected and envied the concise, simple explanation, even though he still had questions. He suddenly felt eighteen again, asking for fatherly advice—or maybe twelve, ashamedly asking for a teacher's help with an easy concept.

"But how are you so certain?"

"How can I *not* be certain?" D snapped back. "I saw it firsthand. I lived it. It's not some blind faith. It's who I am."

D-Tay wasn't flashing frustration at the question but flashing through memories of his years in foster care, the lost connection with his siblings, his all-but-nonexistent parents. Hollis's initial coaching lessons, followed by his letters, texts, and mentorship, got him through all that, then through college to his career.

"I'm grateful for my opportunity, Oskie, and I *will* pay Hollis's help forward. Not out of duty but because it's right, and it's fun, man!" D-Tay turned the volume down a little. "Look, I learned from the best, just like you. I find a need and fill it. That's purpose. And when there's a need that happens to require what I'm good at, when I can actually feel Hollis's lessons being passed on and put to use, that purpose melds into passion. It becomes your voice in this world. It really is that simple. Don't overthink it."

Oskie felt a little scolded but not enough to sound a full retreat. "I got a grip on gratitude, D. You know I loved him too." He paused and winced, trying to be sure before going further. "I just don't always have a handle on the needs I'm supposed to fill or if my work or life fills any at all. Feels just a charade somedays, a charade we just act out until the grave."

And that, as Oskie had suspected, launched D-Tay into a sermon of his own.

"Dude! It really is all about the three bones—wishbone, backbone, funny bone. I know it is fourth-grade level stuff from Hollis, but it's still true. It works.

"All three are connected, but you're only firing on two out of three. You are the hardest of workers at everything, and you know how to have fun ... even if sarcastic or ironic while unhappy man, you're hilarious.

"But your wishbone is flat-out weak. Passion and vision, the stuff of wishes, requires you to feel. You can't think your way to it. You have to allow yourself to *feel* passion. It's not an intellectual endeavor. You gotta let your heart out, man."

Oskie sighed, now feeling not a little scolded but a little stupid. D-Tay had restated Hollis's most preferred proverb, one Oskie had heard his whole life, including one of the first limericks he had stopped on when first skimming through the book.

[Journal Page 51]

Need three bones to stay on top, to make use of life's tide.
Wishbone, backbone, and funny bone help you keep your stride.

Want what you get.
Think, laugh, and sweat.

Have a vision, work hard at it, and enjoy the ride.

D-Tay allowed Oskie his sigh but was going to let him have it anyway.

"Show me a man without a strong wishbone, and I'll see a man who refuses to let himself truly want something or believe in it. He refuses to put his whole heart and faith into something and invest himself. To really go after it.

"That, if I'm forced to pick, is *you*, my man. And I get it. You've lost a lot. But all the hard work and kindness in the world will lack luster until you shine your heart on it. I've seen your heart, and it's phenomenal when on blast. But right now you're me twenty or thirty years ago, staying detached. 'Courteous indifference,' I call it. That way no one can catch you. I've been there. There's pride in that. But you know what I learned? The guy who can't be caught also cannot catch any joy or anyone for himself either. And all pride and no joy is a dead end. I learned it the hard way."

D-Tay paused some for effect but also perhaps some for mercy. This was his friend after all who had slumped against the scorer's table while listening … who had become the Tin Man.

"Try not to sweat it, okay? We all have questions from time to time. I know even Hollis struggled to keep the faith some. But his basic premise was right. And I can tell you from experience on both sides, *feeling* is the same as thinking in that it's a habit, but it's also the exact opposite, in that too much thinking can smother the ability to feel. That's why people meditate, I think. Gotta get your mind out of your heart, and you'll *feel* your passion. You'll find your needs to fill."

Ever the good coach, D-Tay ended the lesson on an uptick, offering the sweetness of hope to the bitterness of the pill. The right approach is always, yes, we have a weakness, but if we can do *this* or *that*, we can fix it.

A few seconds of silence ensued. Both men staring off at Turbo on the side goal, following the sound of the bouncing ball, and both were thinking, *Please*, one for *Please forgive my weakness* and the other for *Please forgive any harshness*, followed by "Thank you," both as in thank you for our friendship. Much like D-Tay's speech, both men got this silent message too.

"So, speaking of needs ..."

Oskie smiled wryly and segued them back from macro to micro, to the real reason he had come to the gym.

"I need to know if you want to go see Boo again this week. Elly stopped by today and needs to reserve a time for us. I'd like to go together and will try to roll with anytime you choose, but I told Elly Saturday morning is best for me."

Oskie anticipated a quick yes but raised an eyebrow as D-Tay pulled out his phone to start a text.

"You checking schedules with Mary Beth?"

"Not at all, my man!" D exclaimed. "I'm texting Boo to tell him we'll be up there this weekend!"

D explained that he had shipped Boo a burner phone through Elly and had been texting with him, just like Hollis had done for D.

"That was a much easier question! Seeing Boo is good stuff for us all around. You should have led with that!"

D-Tay had finally fully shifted from coach to comedian. This was a post-practice coach's session after all.

"And speaking of good stuff! Lemme get this straight. You're telling me that Elly just bebopped in unannounced to talk to you about Boo? To give you a message for me? And I'm right here? Just up the street? The same place she came to pick up that phone for Boo?

"I'm no lawyer, my good fellow, but even I could cross-examine that!"

Oskie now slithered a step or two from the scorer's table, but D still had him in his sights.

"If I was a prosecutor, I could surmise her motive and conclude she was making an opportunity. Guess question is, are you gonna conspire with her to commit the crime?"

D-Tay cackled, amusing himself with this visual.

"My dad doesn't do crime. He punishes it."

Turbo interrupted, unaware of his perfect timing. In his world, his boyhood hunger had finally usurped his crush on the cheerleaders. No matter the reason, Oskie put his arm around Turbo as a much-needed escape from D's interrogation.

"See D-Tay? At least someone has his mind right."

Oskie and Turbo trekked toward the gym door, but D wouldn't be deterred, even turning Turbo's comment into a prop to drive home his point.

"Oh yeah, I see it. That little joker is more right that he will ever know. Punishment instead of participation, eh? Think about those words a second." D-Tay put his hand on Oskie's back and followed them out. "One of us could twist that phrase to cover much more than work. Maybe try it on some personal matters? Go on, I dare ya. That phrase is not just about crime. That's a personal motto 'round here, doncha think? Unless … ahem … that is … you actually plan to ask her out."

Oskie knew what D-Tay meant, knew he was right, and even knew he was funny, but he knew most of all to keep walking, not to respond, not to either reaffirm or retaliate, both of which would only poke the humorous D bear further. He was on a roll.

"Hey, man." D-Tay squeezed Oskie's shoulder to stop him at the door after Turbo had walked on through. "You know I'm playing on Elly, right, but you really need to take your heart out for a spin. I meant *all* that. And if she makes your heart spin a little, then I say, take her out too."

And there it was … the perfect summation for dessert after the whole spiel that was the meal. D had really evolved his coaching skills and even added the cherry on top, like that perfect steal and dunk that so often caps off a close basketball game. You don't need it to win, but it is exactly what the fans want and need to go home extra happy, extra whole.

"Let me remind you, my friend, that you were nicknamed for smiling all the time. You remember that? I just think you lost it somewhere or maybe let the world take it? How 'bout you find that guy again for both of us."

— 15 —

PARTY OF ONE

Oskie woke the next morning, walked CP, then got Turbo off to school, just like any other Thursday, but it was no such thing. It was Annie's birthday, though he was still uncertain whether people celebrated births after they were dead. Seemed a bit obtuse, perhaps more appropriate to mark the day of death, the day the other resident ghosts welcomed in the new member to their underground venue. Regardless, like every Mother's Day and Thanksgiving and Christmas since she had died, Oskie got in his truck for a twenty-fifth annual trek to the Emerling Creek Graveyard to say hi to his mom.

He embraced the butterflies in his stomach, such turbulence being the toll for time with his memories of Annie. It was no different from air travel, when a sudden bounce or jolt of turbulence awakened a passenger to the reality of the unsupported tube careening across the sky; milestone moments on a calendar awaken a motherless child to his or her loss and helplessness about it, that he or she is flying without a net and afraid. So children who suddenly lose a parent turn to daily routine, to being *busy*, just like an in-flight movie, to create amnesia from what they know. They choose that amnesia to beat down the anxiety. Those are the two options. And within that airspace of life is the child's limbo, the fault line between two opposing cliffs, the past he or she wants and the pain relief he or she needs. The child hangs there, a hand clinging to both ledges, unwilling to let go of one and unable to let go of the other.

Holidays and special events such as Annie's birthday erased the façade of Oskie's rituals, like that week between Christmas and New Year's when most folks cannot pin down what day it is. The hustle slows, and the mind is vulnerable to those voices and visions usually kept in the corner and ignored.

Oskie had taken the day off work, out of respect and love for his mother, of course, but what real choice did he have? His walls of protective programming down, he was compelled to erect new patterns in their place. Oskie had suspected such instincts drove most New Year's resolutions, that it wasn't so much the turn of the calendar but more the urge to replace the mind's insulation from the pensive thoughts seeping in. People build those palaces in their minds with every holiday tradition or New Year plan, most mundane and draining, such as countless Christmas cards that are literally garbage moments after they are read, or trying to eat three meals with three different relatives in three different towns on the same day, followed by the terrible night's sleep on a couch or floor in an overcrowded, under air-conditioned home. Oskie identified with such nonsense, walking betwixt the tombstones toward Annie's cross-shaped one, where he would share a conversation with still, silent concrete, but he grabbed any port in such limbo. A person just needs something to do.

"Happy birthday, Mom."

Oskie propped open a lawn chair and began to rifle through his usual bag of goodies for her. He set out a bottle of sparkling water—"dainty water," as she would have called it—and a bag of little clementine oranges, forever her favorite snack, on top of her cross. The items wouldn't survive the graveyard's weekend landscaping and maintenance crews, but again, he needed the tangible task and solace in sticking to birthday protocol. So many things people do for love and family lack common sense, but there's just no acceptable alternative you can stomach. They just cannot *not* do it. Cannot even picture it. So Oskie would sacrifice a few birthday grocery gifts. He also pulled two glasses from the bag and poured two shots of bourbon, sitting one glass alongside the oranges and downing the other in a gulp. No need to waste his portion.

"I still remember, Mom. Thank you."

Oskie kept his whispered sentences short to preempt any tears and occupied his mouth with a second drink. He did remember her, starting with the echo of the trains across the street from the house on North Second Street. His mind recalled footage of Annie and his five-year-old self dropping any chore to peer out the house's rear kitchen window at the passing trains. There was Annie teaching him to dance to old-school '70s Barry Manilow or Bee Gees, then finger-combing his exhausted, sweaty hair until he rocked to sleep. Annie adored her "little Cucibini," her made-up name for kindergarten Oskie derived from the coquina shells they had found together on the beach. Oskie's card catalog continued to an older section, where Annie was later in charge of the travel entertainment on long drives to games. She was the one inventing a game out of road signs or license plates, parlaying a stray word into an ironic laugh, or simply pointing out the scenery, the mountains, and colors, all the little flavors of life. Oskie almost smiled as the second shot of bourbon reached his belly, since these mental souvenirs were the warmup pitches, the captain's jokes, and the flight attendants' small talk before the plane's velocity clamped you back in your seat.

"I'm sorry, Mom. Please forgive me."

I'm sorry, the most banal and useless of all words repeated at a time of loss, yet for those who mean them, they are the only two that fit. The sorrow comes like ocean waves, deep and multilayered, spitting out the words over and over again. Oskie was indeed sorry. Sorry for his mom, that she wasn't there and had been shorted a full life to enjoy. Sorry to his mom that he hadn't gotten home in time that day, that he couldn't save her motionless body, which he had found on the bathroom floor. Sorry that he still needed her, that maybe that meant he hadn't learned enough from her, hadn't appreciated her presence and gifts, hadn't lived a life worthy of having had such a mother. And sorry for himself, that she couldn't hear him, and there was nothing he could do about it but wipe his tears and pour another drink.

"I love you, Mom."

Oskie hesitated to gather his breath and the belief that she knew this. He knew he felt *something*, a longing for her presence, but the inability to show her cheapened it in his mind, disgraced her. This had to be *different*, more than missing a lost puppy or friend. He cried again at now the root of the eternal anxiety for a kid left behind. It's the separation, the love without an outlet, the unplugged sensation in place of the greatest power you had felt.

"Tell me what to do, Mom. *Anything*. How do I love you from here?"

Annie's concrete cross responded with silence. Oskie stared some, soaking it in, then gathered himself to go before remembering the limerick book in the bag.

"Hey, I forgot, Mom." He opened to an earmarked page. "You may have known these already, or maybe he's found you by now? Hollis wrote you a good one.

[Journal Page 55]

I still see you though you're gone, and I hope you're anxious to be on your way.
Vivid are your heart and eyes, so I'm destined to look for you here each day.

Don't get to decide on love or death,
Not a heart's first beat nor lung's last breath,

But I'm not sad, just grateful, for you the tears are such a small price to pay."

He read the limerick aloud in full despite only the birds chirping in return.

"I'm proud of you, Mom. And want you proud of me. Hope you know."

Oskie was honest with her always, but pride was also the only way he could cope with the anxiety. He was indeed proud and grateful that of all the mothers in the world, he had gotten sixteen years with her. But even that recognition amplified uncertainty of how to ever earn or deserve her, and all Oskie could offer was the promise to see her—or at least her graveyard cross—again soon.

Oskie spent a few hours milling about town to empty his mind, and by five thirty that afternoon, he had succeeded in recalibrating. He had a bloodstream of coffee and was essentially a walking, anaesthetized wound of a man. He had traded tears and hurt for things to do, and next on the list was the district championship basketball game at Wilmington High. It was still two hours before tipoff, but Oskie had multiple anxieties requiring early attendance.

Oskie waved at Turbo, who was already in ball boy attire and taking a few shots on the empty visitors' end of the gym. D-Tay nodded from the home side, watching his troops shoot around and go over some last-minute repetitions. The opponents' bus hadn't yet arrived, and neither had the officials. Aside from a couple of janitors sweeping through the bleachers and the PA announcer testing the microphone, the forum was in Oskie's favorite form before a game: quiet. He would have welcomed the respite anyway after the morning he'd had, but on any day, he remained forever uneasy with the crowd when not coaching. Hell, even when he was in coaching mode, the short trip from locker room to sideline was excruciating. Having grown up within the sanctuary of the games themselves and having heard enough ignorance and malice from the spectators, he distrusted any eyes his might meet.

Oskie thankfully crawled to a bleacher spot hidden beneath the scoreboard at the entrance, a third-row seat with a great view of both the game and home team sideline, where he would be able to see Turbo and even hear D-Tay in action. It also provided cover as the crowd would file in toward their center court seats, leaving him largely unnoticed as they passed by. D-Tay followed the team down the steps and tunnel beneath Oskie and the bleachers. He winked at his friend on the way, appearing confident, like any coach before the big game, and the next time he and the team surfaced, it would be time for battle.

Oskie rested his head against the gym wall, still expelling the emotions of the day. His thoughts reverted to coaching, always a well-timed, tactile diversion to beguile some time. In particular, Oskie centered on D-Tay and what words he might be offering twelve teenage boys for motivation in the dressing room below. A good coach is part conversion expert, part con artist, meaning the team must wholly believe in the operation; and to do that, they must believe their coach believes, but that same coach must reserve a small pathway in his philosophy for the very real possibility that the team could lose. Like poker, a coach must sell the bluff completely but leave himself outs in case he gets called. Or like a lawyer, no matter what the witness answers, the jury sees the lawyer take it exactly as expected and twisted to support the overall theory of the case. Expect the best, prepare for the worst. If not, the coach who completely sells out cannot revive the team after disappointment. The coach's message goes sideways, and the team loses its faith.

Oskie's confidence and admiration for D-Tay's coaching skills had grown in the last decade since they had joined forces. Oskie knew himself more of a pessimistic protector of player psyches, and he knew D-Tay was more apt to believe the fairy-tale ending could—and would—happen. There was absolutely nothing wrong with that, and there were many ways to skin a win.

Wilmington faced an uphill climb tonight against favored Tybee County, and Oskie could hear D at the top of the tunnel, dusting off Hollis's old gas station direction reference for the boys at just the right time.

"The world is negative and beats you down at every turn, gentlemen," yelled D. "Even the old codger at the gas station tells you to 'go down three blocks and turn at the red light.' Why does everyone expect it to be red? Why not 'go turn at the green light,' eh? We don't have to think like the world does, gentlemen, and we don't have to be or do what they say either. Let's go show 'em!"

Oskie's eyes smiled at the sight of Hollis's face and voice from years gone by. He had no idea what D-Tay would say to them later if the world's thoughts on this particular game were correct, but he just took the moment to relish the coaching cake and not fret over how D had baked it. He was a grown-ass coach, and he'd figure it out.

"Yo, Booas! Let me guess. You were here so early you didn't even have to pay!"

Belle smacked him on the thigh and sat down beside him. The gym was pretty packed at that point, but hers was the first face in the crowd he cared to see.

"You act like you know me."

Oskie's words took in her love and tapped back some of his own. Like a puppy pawing playfully with his litter mates, she was his little sis, and he was happy to see her.

"I don't care if you're cheap and want to beat the box office. Just don't be coming early to hide out from the fans." She was clearly revved up for the game and spilling over on Oskie. "I've told you for years. Half the hacks up here think you're the best ever. The other half don't even know there's a game going on."

Oskie heard her advice for the umpteenth time but pretended to ignore it, also for the umpteenth time. He imitated a coach enthralled by the dunks and cheerleader stunts during pregame warmups, but his gaze had actually detoured through the maze of activity to Elly's face in the bleachers across the court.

"I'm going to run to the bathroom and grab a drink before it starts." Belle was already on her way as she asked, "Whatcha want?"

"No worries, sis, but if you bring a water, I'll take it."

Belle vanished in a pile of people gathered by the door leading to the concession stand, or maybe she was abducted by aliens. Oskie's eyes had no idea, as they caromed occasionally to check Turbo's ball boy action but stayed mostly on Elly, whose vision appeared similarly situated. She glanced back and forth between Oskie in the stands and her daughter, Leigh, on the floor, since Leigh and the other middle school cheerleaders were partnering with the high school girls for the big game. Elly finally broke the staring contest by pointing to her phone, as in *Check yours, man!*

The pertinent portions read as follows:

Elly	**Oskie**
You get up with D-Tay?	
	It's on for Saturday. 11ish?
Sounds good. I'll confirm tomorrow.	
	Anything going on for you after?
You mean Saturday?	
	Yes, ma'am.
	Got two tickets to UK/ UofL. Fourth row.
	But just a party of one over here.
How can I say no to that?	
	That was the idea. ☺
	Even if you only go for the game, win-win.
Honey, I've seen plenty of basketball games.	
	So that's a yes to one more?
That's a yes to YOU.	

Oskie looked up from his phone just in time to accept a bottle of water from Belle's outstretched arm.

"Thanks, Belle," he said as she sat down. "You were right, by the way."

She had no clue what he meant, but just as she'd said, there he sat in the stands, not even knowing there was a game going on, at least not the game they had come to watch.

"Always am, Booas." She didn't care what. She just knew. "When you gonna learn?"

Oskie didn't know about learning, but he was suddenly trying.

— 16 —

Thought We'd Win

Oskie had barely sipped the water before he wished it was vodka. He was immediately disconcerted, unable to recall his last real date or the reasons for his impulsiveness.

"What have I done?"

He smiled and resignedly slid Belle the open text thread on his cell phone, doing it gingerly the way people do when nauseous, when flustered at the thought of *any* further movement.

"Well, why doncha look at you, Booas?" Belle returned the phone. "If I had known the master was at work, I would have skipped the bathroom to watch."

Belle was joking about his past, when Oskie had always kept his romantic pursuits to himself to help his present, in which Oskie was readily recoiling from his Saturday commitment. She could see it on his face. He had clamped himself in a roller coaster, slowly climbing up the first hill, and he wanted to stop the world for a second or perhaps reverse it about ten minutes.

He put his head back against the wall and tried not to grimace, but that's what he felt. It was the weight of second-guessing. The brain was barely built for the decisions we make, let alone when we constantly try to review them twice.

"Isn't *she* a lucky bird?" Belle laughed, doing what one does when seeing someone falter; grab an arm and lift the person up. "She'll have a great time she'd *never* get otherwise, and you'll have fun showing her that."

Oskie noted the halftime score, good guys down by eight. Doable but a high degree of difficulty. He could relate at the moment, seeing his Saturday to come just the same.

"Ya know, if I can go heavy a moment, I think Mom would smile at you for going. It doesn't have to be a life-defining moment, just you treating another person to some fun and kindness, the way Mom always did."

Oskie really tuned into Belle this time, absorbing thoughts of Annie, even while still facing toward the halftime show. He saw little Leigh proudly adding the most crooked of cartwheels to the cheerleader performance. Elly was laughing and shaking her head as Oskie's eyes found her across the way. His phone buzzed, and her text said, "Kids … seemed like a good idea at the time."

He couldn't help but tee-hee to that, and he couldn't help but feel her playfulness settle his stomach. She really was pretty cool. And he couldn't help but agree that Annie would likely have approved, since she had always wanted joy for her son and for him to at least *try* to find it. And he couldn't help but notice Belle's smack-talking posture as she read the text and his reaction.

"Is this where I remind you I'm always right? Oh wait! I just did that a minute ago."

The game and Wilmington's season ended a couple of quarters later but not for lack of resistance. D-Tay never learned to go down easy, and players always resemble their coach's personality. "Association is assimilation," as Hollis would have said, or "You become what you hang around." Still, a tourney game is a study in extremes, and a loss brings so much sudden death, most of all to the 100 percent belief that was in that locker room just ninety minutes before. D would have tears to mop up and lockers to clean out, so Oskie escorted Belle to her car and then shepherded Turbo toward home.

"I really thought we would win, Dad."

That was all Turbo said on a somber ride across town. Oskie let the words sit there. Coaching had taught him the art of silence. There would be pain, tears, and some messy hearts and faces, even for the ball boy in his back seat, but that was okay. The old weight room saying "No pain, no gain" actually applied best to the emotional side of sports, though it was always hard for a coach or a parent or—in Oskie's case on this night—*both* to allow that hurtful seed to plant and grow. You want to wipe tears, instantly replace any bad with good, and explain everything away. Not tonight.

"Let's talk it out tomorrow, Turbo," Oskie offered as he walked Turbo and CP upstairs to bed. "It's better to see the how and why things happened after some rest. And besides, we have a busy Friday ahead."

All that was true. Perspective is proportionate to distance. And they had travel team practice at six a.m., then Turbo to school, and Oskie to court, then game night over at D-Tay's and Mary Beth's. A full day for sure, whether aged forty or ten. The unsaid was also true. After the emotional ups and downs of the day, Oskie just needed to close up shop early. He had fallen into sadness over Annie, then climbed out of it, only then to run and jump off the next cliff on a whim. He was no different from Turbo and would try to take his own advice. The how and why and what to do next would be best analyzed when the sun came up.

A spattering of snow, CP snapping up a treat, and two bleary-eyed boys with bags packed climbing into the truck for practice at 5:45 a.m. The usual Friday, until Oskie and Turbo turned on the lights in the gym to find D-Tay already there, dripping with sweat.

Turbo dropped his gear to rebound for D, who was finishing up an hour of self-flagellation with a round of jump shots. Oskie set up for practice, wholly unsurprised, as he and D-Tay shared the same postseason shape. Liquid. To make penance for mistakes, exorcise your anguish and absolve your regret; they turned their human form into as much sweat as possible. This was D-Tay's morning after, and he obviously couldn't sleep, so he had come early to make his peace with the loss.

Oskie did do a double take though on all the laughter he was hearing at the other end of the gym. Turbo and D had devolved into a game of "knockout" with accompanying giddiness. Usually, the big-loss grieving process was pain, sweat, clarity, then resolve … all solemn, almost angry. But D-Tay was amply upbeat.

"What's gotten into *you*, sir? Did you and I both attend the same game last night?"

Oskie half-expected some kind of new pre-workout powder. D-Tay was a ball of energy, patting everyone on the back, high-fiving kids as they warmed up with simple catch, mouthing enthusiasm to anyone in earshot.

"*Happy* got into me, boss man, and you are welcome to check your court files, but you will find that *happy* is not a crime."

D-Tay was hopping around, helping everyone. Much like the old Bugs Bunny cartoon where he plays every position on the baseball field alone, he could coach this practice himself. The kids were snickering, the sweat drops flying, and it was a symphony of sport, orchestrated by a one-man band. Oskie took the gifted energy as it came, but seriously, was his friend on crack?

"You know I'm on your wagon, sir, but you mind filling me in? *Before* you're sent for a drug test at school this morning?"

Oskie interrupted with his comedic inquiry only with the kids at a water break, when D was still enough to see, one notch below a blur.

"I'll do you one better, Big O! Or better yet, I'll do you three like Hollis!"

He was actually shooting baskets, and not missing, between sentences at each breath.

"We had a great season. Better than expected. We see Boo Saturday, and he's been texting me. He seems okay. And maybe ... my best friend is saying there's a chance!"

Oskie's eyes bulged. How did he know? Anybody else, and maybe even D-Tay with any other delivery, would have set Oskie back on his heels, forced his retreat to his preclusive cave. But after momentary beats for D to catch his breath from all the talking, the two just guffawed, one knowing he had nailed the facts, the other knowing there was no defending this brand of D-Tay. If you can't beat 'em ...

Practice flew by in its "D-Taffeinated" state, and otherwise helpless to his supersonic partner, Oskie's newly created adjective was officially his only contribution to the session. He did get D to fill in one blank though. Elly had stopped D-Tay after the game and discussed Saturday, mentioning both the likely eleven a.m. Boo visit and then her trip with Oskie afterward. That's how he knew, and that's how he got over the loss so soon.

The frenetic Friday never found its brakes after its fast start. By midmorning, Oskie was already knee deep into his third coffee and his fifth of fifteen cases with Judge Pete in juvenile court, and he would have imagined D-Tay still dancing around his fifth-grade math class *if* he had a moment to spare.

"How 'bout these next two, Oskie? You think you might talk to the Simpson boys and get to the bottom of their latest school stunt?"

Judge Pete handed Oskie their files and nodded toward the conference room, where young William and Michael Simpson, ages twelve and ten respectively, awaited their fate. Both were already regular court attendees, and both had open probation cases with Oskie. Sometimes in cases involving minor charges and ongoing probation, Oskie had a knack for compromise and saving the court time. They'd still need their public defender present, but often the kids and their attorney would let their guard down for Oskie as opposed to a prosecutor. Oskie would still recommend punishment to Judge Pete when appropriate, but it helped that his primary objective was the child's best interests and not the child thrown under the jail.

"Oh, and sir." Judge Pete waved him back up in private. "You find a mate yet for that second ticket on Saturday?"

Oskie looked up from the files to Judge P., his scoffing face meaning every bit of *You too? You cannot be serious.* Pete never looked more like Santa, with a wink that already knew whether Oskie had been naughty or nice and what was wrapped under the tree. Oskie pleaded the fifth and went on his way. He knew Judge P. was just happy for him, and D-Tay had already hammered home the invincibility of happy, so he just had to withstand the storm.

Judge had pulled the right string using Oskie on the Simpsons. There was ten-year-old Michael, the muscle of the operation, who had boosted older brother, William—only half Michael's size but the brains of the outfit and known locally as Wilmington's own Billy the Kid—through a school window. Then Michael had *tried* to catch a microwave thrown down to him, but the oven had obviously been too much for him and had been damaged beyond repair. So you had burglary (going through the window) and criminal mischief (destruction of the oven), both misdemeanors, for two kids grabbing an oven for their home that didn't have one. And as you might expect, there were no concerned parents at the conference, just two kids facing the music alone.

Michael was found with scratch marks on his hands from the bobbled appliance; he had confessed when the cops came knocking. Again, the kid was more brawn than brains. But not Billy. The mastermind maintained it had been only a one-man job, done only by Michael, and he held on tightly to the strings of Michael's loyal silence. But cutting the strings was elementary. Oskie dropped an obvious untruth, which would interest Michael enough to correct it, nabbing his brother in the process. In this case, Oskie "limericked" his way to the legal truth.

[Oskie's Legal Pad]

Oskie: "Michael, cops found the broken oven, but what of the TV?"

Michael: "No such thing. We just swiped the oven, just like you said, Billy?"

Billy: Elbowing Michael, "Shut up, dummy!"

Billy: "Now I'm up the river with you, see?"

Michael: A pause, then: "Hey, Billy, think we'll still get to keep the TV?"

Mystery solved, easy peasy, especially for one with Oskie's experience. In any number of better lives, the budding Simpson crime family could be playing travel baseball or answering math problems at the front of the class, but their world was far less fun, their needs far more basic. Their counsel agreed to extended probation and community service at the school. With the threat to humanity averted, Oskie was doodling limericks the rest of the day. Maybe happy was contagious.

The rest of the day sped downhill until Oskie coasted to a stop in D-Tay's driveway by six thirty that evening. Non-football Fridays meant Turbo rode home with D after school for video game wars, and Mary Beth would feed the troops their favorites by seven p.m., thin-crust pizza for the child and cobb, seafood, and steak salads for the adults, though Turbo typically had to smack sneaky hands away from his pizza. Oskie's arrival would complete the crew and signal the weekend, starting with grown-man Ping-Pong in the garage before dinner—two out of three between the most competitive chaps to relax. Not a chance.

"My man!" D-Tay said as he slammed the first point. "I am excited for you! Worst case, just a super-fun Saturday, but best case—this one is worthy of *real* consideration."

D-Tay bobbed and weaved just as he had twelve hours ago. He made Oskie feel old instantly, in both energy and the topic of conversation, but D was still amped up and dominating, in both Ping-Pong points and punchy words.

"Yeah," moaned Oskie, "consider where to rank this on my Hall of Fame of mistakes?" Oskie's return of serve, like his deflection of the Elly talk, was pitiful.

"You kill me sometimes, O. I'd say you really have *no idea* on love. *None.*" D-Tay swiped a winner Oskie couldn't reach to go up 8–4. The comment stung some too.

"Okay, Mr. Big Shot, I'll bite. Explain it to me." Oskie's frustrated serve went wide off the table. "How do you even know *you're* in love. Lay it out like I'm four years old."

"Oh my." D-Tay's jaw dropped to gesture. "You dare disrespect the champ?" After a little resistance from Oskie at 17–14, D reeled off four straight points to finish off game one while his mouth watered at the love potion of words about to spew.

"Allow me to paint this picture for you." He served and rocked to the rhythm of his words to start game two. "You'll know you're in real love when you see no holes. There's not one thing about Mary Beth—mind, body, or spirit—that I would change."

A netted serve failed to dissuade him. He scraped up the ball and served up some more.

"And at the same time, you no longer see holes in yourself, because she fills up all of you. Every curve you're missing is one she has. It's true comfort … comfort you don't understand until you feel it, that what you are is exactly what they need you to be. Her presence makes sense of all my bullshit. All the stuff I went through molded me to fit her—right person, right time, and most of all, the right kinda love."

Oskie served down 11–13, gagging a bit on the love … and the losing. He'd have gladly agreed to a double date or even to fall in love at that point if it would shush D up or at least somehow help him tie the score.

"You know me, man. I *have* to win," D's flurry continued. "I have to love better than all those chumps we know. Just have to. If love is the Olympics, I'm winning the decathlon, and I'm taking gold in every event. And yet if I do all of that, if I love her harder than any man that ever lived, I know it will never be all the love that she deserves."

Another of Oskie's backhands went wide, setting up game point. It was all but over, and perhaps rightfully so, since even Oskie had to admit that last comment was cool.

"Seriously, O," D said as he held the last serve a second, "I want you to feel it. It's inimitable. You're inspired to give every ounce of yourself to them, compelled by overwhelming emotion, and yet you're a willful volunteer, laser focused by a mind without doubt. She makes my heart blurry and my head clear at the same time. And I had never known either before her.

"To be continued!"

D-Tay's emphatic ace ended the two-game sweep, and his touchdown dance assured there was plenty mo' love lesson, and Ping-Pong later, if Oskie wanted some. "Time to eat. Nothing makes a man hungrier than lovin' … and winnin'."

— 17 —

A Done Deal

F riday had undoubtedly been fun, from the early-morning practice all the way to midnight, when Oskie had bourboned himself to sleep in his recliner, Turbo and CP tucked away upstairs. Oskie could physically feel, intellectually know, and spiritually embrace a good time. His fun with family or friends, like game night with the D-Tay and Mary Beth, was just as real for him as anyone else. But just as real was the dread and agitation he woke with early that Saturday morning. Oskie was capable of fishing for fun, but it was always catch and release.

That's the game depression plays. It can start physically, from a hormonal or chemical imbalance, or emotionally as with Oskie, from repeated trauma or loss. But while those larger events initially ground you, it's the thought traps that provide the quicksand to keep you down. Hollis had once broken down depression for Oskie in its simplest terms. The thoughts *dupe* your mind, *press* down on your soul, and convince your spirit to *shun* the world or to think the world shuns you. Dupe, press, shun. Cute. But unhelpful and, to a deep, dark mind like Oskie's, wholly unnecessary, for that is the point. The facts don't matter. They are as indisputable as the fun. Oskie lucidly dissected depression at its depths, but he still couldn't cut the cord constricting his thoughts. His thoughts circled back to the hurt, an ever-tightening circle of hate of past pain and anger that it would just happen again, and in that web of immense pain, the depressed mind released everything—reason, facts, emotion, connection. Loneliness became his favorite place to be.

"Did you hit a snag?"

D-Tay broke the silence in the truck about twenty minutes in. Oskie's sigh in response told him all he needed to know.

"You think the Cats will win?"

D opted for the safest ground he could find among two diehard Kentucky basketball fans. "Just gotta get it over with."

Oskie didn't want to talk about it. He didn't want anything. He was struggling with the day and date ahead, his mind not wanting to cash the check his heart had already written. D-Tay rode another mile before he could no longer hold it in.

"So you're really gonna ghost your way through this?"

D knew he was picking at a scab, knew he likely shouldn't. Like the teen in the mirror with a pimple, it rarely ended well. Oskie walled him off with his driver's arm, leaning toward his door, body language for *You can go kick rocks.* But D was just too exasperated to let it go. At some point, friends and family of an addict—be it liquor, crack, or thought traps—grow angry, and they just can't lay it down. Oskie was sick of talking about it only a smidge more than D was sick of watching it.

"Don't you *ever* get tired? Tired of just going through the motions?" D-Tay tried to keep a compassionate tone as Oskie's eyes darted wildly in agitation. "Just seems like from an intellectual standpoint, when you're stuck in the same rut, that you might try a new approach to things? Maybe just *try* it?"

"Let's just not talk about it. How about we try that?"

Oskie was seething, and his blood pressure escalated further, knowing that his vehement rejection of trying a new approach actually proved D-Tay's point correct.

"I'm really not trying to coach you, O. But I've seen you happy. I know it's in you. I've seen you running around crazy after touchdowns, getting hugs from Turbo, laughing to tears with me and Mary Beth while playing cards. I know you know what joy is, and it just doesn't make sense that you would not want to make that for yourself. You walk around, caring for everyone every day, but you actually *choose* to not be part of anything. You're so freakin' smart, Oskie. You've always been so much smarter than me. So this is not some hokey self-help talk. I'm honestly just asking. Do you think your ghost status is all you're worthy of? That it's your destiny to stay disengaged? So much that you sabotage a chance before it starts?"

D-Tay had described the deception of depression, the equivalence of a functional alcoholic. In so many moments on so many days, Oskie seemed just fine. But he was still captive, and until ready to leave on his own accord, he would actually defend his captor.

"You just can't tell me it ultimately makes a difference. None of it."

Oskie begrudgingly cracked open the door to an intellectual debate, but he already knew the foregone conclusion, having covered this ground a hundred times in his head, and he was a bit angry inside that he had to redo it, even for his dear friend. Oskie split his mind into two people, one sword and one shield—one to cordially spar with D on the outside, the other to guard the fortress of his beliefs on the inside. Those beliefs would never be touched, and that very maneuver that felt so normal—to keep others at bay—again proved the exact disorder in play.

"Let's say I score all the touchdowns." Oskie rubbed the back of his neck to keep calm. Outwardly Oskie didn't need anger. He had the facts on his side. "Say that I'm a Hall of Famer or even an NFL coach, the greatest ever. I am wealthy beyond measure, see every country, and date any and every pretty girl. It means nothing. Just achievements in a made-up social structure to satisfy our ego, to convince ourselves we are more than ants on a rock in space. We're still only dust at the end of it, and like George Carlin said, we're all two, maybe three generations, from being erased entirely."

What inward Oskie held back from this three-way conversation was the lifetime of proof he had for his premise. He could have spewed the venom of his experience. He had indeed given his heart to teams and touchdowns, but all that winning produced only molded metal trophies in the attic. He was a good kid, did what he was told, and tried to please everyone, but he was never good enough for the dissatisfied mob. He gave his heart to his family and friends, but it had been too little to save Pookie and too late to save his mom. Four years at a small college, recruiting and coaching other wannabe quarterbacks to their pipe dreams, another four years in the National Guard reclaiming unattainable peace in the Middle East, two years building houses and chasing religions with the hopelessly poor in Central Africa, all before relenting and returning to his current courthouse cage … a career to hypnotize himself with kids in need, just like D, but not one significant, lasting feat in the bunch.

"I'm not disagreeing with our mortality, Oskie. I hear the clock ticking too."

D-Tay was walking a fine line, trying to reboot his friend without shutting him down. But it seemed Oskie's thoughts were stuck, the little blue circle on the monitor just spinning and spinning without end.

"But doesn't it seem like you're closing your mind to possibilities? You instinctively argue against the meaning of everything without actually weighing what you see and feel. Is it not the kid who dodges vegetables but complains when he's smaller than the other kids? Or like a diehard Republican or Democrat. It's mathematically impossible that one line of thought is always right, but they won't even listen to the other side. Isn't it at least *possible* that the very things you deny yourself as unwanted waste could provide the very missing pieces of truth you're searching for?

"I would just ask you to ask yourself, 'If you've figured it all out, if you've solved life's equations, then why aren't you happy?'"

Inward Oskie smoldered at D-Tay's questioning, the heat on the back of his neck now irresistible. His unspoken reaction was, "You're wrong, way the fuck wrong. You're deluded by emotion, and you've adopted Hollis's philosophy of empathy to justify your own existence, to make sense of the meaningless. You're the one that believes your own bullshit. Not me." Inward Oskie even penned a limerick while simmering in silence.

[Oskie's Inner Voice]

You expect levity, but I stand aghast.
I see your bliss, but I can't ignore the past.

Our ideas will just clash.
I won't dance in this trash.

You can have your fun; leave me alone at last.

"We're almost there, sir."

Outward Oskie spoke up more gracefully, despite the rage within. "I'm glad that you're happy with your life, and I understand you see things differently. What do you say we just agree to disagree for now?"

"Fair enough … my man."

D was the one holding back now. He had battered his friend enough. He wouldn't rub any more salt in the wound he had dug into.

"Just know I'm thankful you talked it out with me, and I want you happy. That's all."

Sometimes in coaching you just flush a bad day. You don't run extra sprints or yell louder or whip the horses harder. It's just not there, and you live to fight another day with rest and a better frame of mind. D would agree to disagree. Either everything matters, or nothing does, and in many ways, they were both right.

~

The Toyota pulled up to St. Vincent's a few minutes early, since the slight tension in the truck after their truce lent itself to more force on the gas pedal. The friends were momentarily frayed but fine. Besides, Boo was waiting.

"Hey, man." D-Tay saw his last shot before Elly arrived and took it. "If you take nothing else I've ever said with you, please hear this, and I'll leave you alone. Something in your heart spoke out to ask Elly to the game today. You were inspired to act. In my experience, inspiration is not a renewable resource, okay? It has an expiration date. It comes and goes without warning, so don't discard it casually. Mary Beth is the source of my greatest joy, but if I had ignored her, she'd be that joy for someone else."

Oskie nodded, his face saying, *Yeah, yeah, yeah.*

Until there she was, heading their way down the long sidewalk from the St. Vincent entrance. Oskie still couldn't put his finger on the source of Elly's power, but her curious style screamed "high voltage" in every direction. She was striking, not a modern-day, paper-doll, billboard knockout, but in a more classic, sensuous way. Even through an otherwise-common game day ensemble, her skin-tight denim jeggings with her black tank top and tunic sweater combo matching her ankle boots, you could picture her sculpted as the ancient Greek statues. It wasn't the getup but how she got up in them. She was smoky, alluring, and the most beautiful thing Oskie had ever seen, even when not trying to be.

Elly moved first to embrace D-Tay, laying her hand gently against Oskie's shoulder on the way. Oskie felt her undeniable electricity shiver him, shocking his system clean of all other thoughts.

"So good to see you, too."

Elly hugged Oskie, briefly holding the back of his head to steady his cheek to hers, and then she turned to lead the men inside to Boo. Oskie followed, honestly thinking of nothing else but the smell of her perfume and the bounce of her walk. Had his mind and memory been "neuralyzed" by some fancy gadget from *Men in Black*? His foreboding had fled, his heart fluttered, and he knew not why. He just knew he wanted her to line back up so he could watch her walk toward them again. D-Tay grabbed the door with a smirk and gently patted Oskie on the back while stepping inside. He managed to hold in the "I told you so."

"Let's gooooooooooo!" Boo had stood chomping at the bit from the visitor's station, and upon sight of the familiar faces, he sprinted down the hall toward the gym with a yelp of elation.

"No worries. I got this one." Oskie picked up his pace, going after Boo. "Y'all have things to talk about."

Oskie had momentarily cleared the clutter between his ears enough to remember he was needed. Both Elly and D seemed a bit squirrely, and she needed to help him weigh his options on Boo. Oskie just needed to help Boo make as many baskets as he could until they were through.

"How's it been going, big man?"

Oskie welcomed the chance to let his guard down with Boo. Inwardly angry Oskie had been lulled to sleep by Elly's charm, and outwardly polished Oskie was weary from fending off D-Tay all morning. He could just *be* with Boo, no bells and whistles, and that was good because kids could spot a fake a mile away. Any adult could be cool with kids so long as he or she was real with them.

"All good, Coach!" Boo looked longer, leaner, and his shots were falling. Oskie, ever the coach, thought this kid may come back a basketball player. "I was really excited when Ms. Elly said you were coming," Boo continued. "Turbo doing any good?"

"Actually," Oskie said, adeptly diverting Boo from baskets to the baggie in his pocket, "Turbo sent you something."

Boo sat against the wall and proceeded to open a card signed by the team at practice the day before. Inside the card was a joke Turbo had written.

> What do you call a bear with no teeth?
> A gummy bear.

Oskie sat down alongside him and pulled from his other pocket a jumbo pack of gummies, Boo's well-known favorite. The two sat there, taking a gummy bear at a time from the bag, facing forward in silence, if you didn't count their sniffles.

As Oskie sat there at St. Vincent's, the emotional extremes of the morning followed by the stillness of the gym with Boo reminded him of why he coached, why he had adopted Turbo, why he worked out daily. Those were all ventures or places where he could just be himself. Full honesty and yet full acceptance. He exhaled deeply, conceding that D-Tay may have presented at least one valid point. Counterfeiting yourself to the world is exhausting. It had been twenty-five years since Annie died and ten years since Pookie. He *was* tired … of the whole complicated gig his life had become. Maybe that's why he gravitated to kids and cringed at things like relationships. He just couldn't stomach the thought of more work, more complications, more pleasing someone, more time on the clock, figuring out who you're supposed to be today.

"Coach Deeeeeeee!"

Boo jumped and beelined to D-Tay, entering the gym. Oskie stood too, looking for facial confirmation of good news from D or Elly.

"We're good to go!" Elly was as excited as anyone, and Oskie noted that made her even cuter. "Case is already on the docket for Monday. Boo's aunt and uncle will be there to sign off. I just needed to know if D-Tay was ready."

Oskie's eyes went to D, as in, *Really? It's a done deal? Mary Beth's in too?*

"I sent you an e-mail, my man. Don't worry about me."

D-Tay's grin grew mischievous. "Just read it later. It will fill you in. I'm gonna hang here with Boo until visiting hours are up, and I'll get the truck back as planned. Just go have fun. Seems you two now have things to talk about."

— 18 —

THE BIG GAME

Oskie stood cautiously outside Elly's car, strangely uncertain of the most chivalrous route to take. He took in the powder-blue Toyota Rav-4, one of the new hybrids. He never paid much attention to cars but noted how much it matched Elly, the best mix of spicy and cool he had seen.

"Well?"

Elly shot him a shrug. "Get in, silly."

Oskie waited for her invitation and then sat down and belted up gingerly, wanting somehow to make every move perfect. She was easing out on the highway as he was easing into the idea of being alone in the car with her for the next ninety minutes or so. He nervously woke his phone and tapped the e-mail from D-Tay in his in-box. It led with the title of "You Da' Man," but then in an all-capped first sentence, it said,

> HEY! IF YOU'RE READING THIS ON YOUR DATE, STOP RIGHT NOW AND PAY ATTENTION TO HER WHILE YOU HAVE A CHANCE! READ THIS AFTER!

Oskie couldn't help but giggle and shoved the phone into the seat between his legs, thankful for the timely manhood tip from his friend.

"Couldn't wait to read D-Tay's e-mail, eh?" Elly wanted in on the joke.

"Yeah, but he's just trying to be funny, emphasis on the word *trying*."

Oskie was further grateful for the icebreaker and decided he would use the topic of D further for the easy conversation. "You didn't take long at St. Vincent's. Is it all settled with Boo?"

"You staying with D-Tay for two hundred dollars, Alex?"

She thought herself cute with her *Jeopardy* reference and in her attempt at humor to calm their nerves. Oskie still felt butterflies, but he agreed with the first part.

"Actually, D did most of the talking, and he said some pretty remarkable things," she said thoughtfully. "He's very ready to be a dad. I figured you guys hashed it out on the way up."

"Not too much." Oskie tried to paraphrase his car ride with D-Tay to sound more romantic than it had been. "Color me selfish, but I guess I was a little preoccupied with *you*, and he was more than happy to rib me about it."

Now he thought himself cute by slipping in a subtle flirtation. She caught it but just smiled ambiguously for now.

"Well, D said it's been weighing on his mind a long while. He said his old coach taught him that a man's heart has room for three kinds of love. There's love of your fellow man, the desire to make the world a better place, which he said he gets through teaching and coaching.

"Then he said there's the love for your mate, and he knows without a doubt that he loves Mary Beth more than *any* man has ever loved *anything*." She smiled softly. "He said it with such conviction ... almost made me cry on that one.

"And then he said the love of family, and that includes the people you're given to start with and the ones you find along the way." She turned to look Oskie in the eye for the first time since getting in the car. "He included you in that, Oskie, and I think he almost cried at that point. He said a man's heart requires you to find those people, your family, and share life with them. And he has no doubt that Boo is part of that family, a kid just like him, perfectly aligned to replace family he's lost over the years and fill open spaces in his heart.

"And then he just said, 'Elly, if I complete all three of those loves, my heart will be full.'"

Oskie couldn't quite recall the first time he had heard about a man's three loves. His guess was a Little League dugout with Hollis around the age of twelve, but he most definitely knew he liked the way he had just heard it best. He spoke up only when he noticed that the melody of her voice had stopped.

"That coach was my dad."

"Really? I wondered." She offered Oskie a chance to engage. "Your dad and D were close?"

Oskie had often been proud of his father and all he had provided, but he had a hard time believing Hollis was reaching down at that moment to help him on this date, though it seemed he was.

"Dad loved him some D-Tay for sure, and he was a man of many words. D's always been a good egg, and I think he was kind of a blank slate when Dad found him. So D-Tay seemed to sponge up everything Dad said over the years. I think Dad filled a gap for D in the same way D was talking to you about Boo.

"I was curious as to Mary Beth's take. Did he mention her at all?"

Oskie had just seen Mary Beth the night before but did slightly wonder if she was on board. She hadn't offered to come to St. Vincent's that morning, and she always played things close to the vest. That was just her way.

"She'll be there Monday at the custody hearing. D said she's excited." Elly grew more animated too. "It sounded like she has the same counseling or coaching gene. They both enjoy kids so much, and D said they both believe the best chance to express all they have to give would be through their own child. They've been about to have their own anyway, so Boo is right on time."

If she was selling them as perfect parents or selling anything else for that matter, Oskie was long since sold. The thought in his head was, *You had me at the* Jeopardy *reference*, but he held that in not to dishonor her with a half-witted joke. He already considered her very presence sacred. On three occasions as she spoke, Oskie had managed to glide his eyes over her profile, watching the choreography of her face. Her mouth outlined words that her eyes filled in with emotion, and he could imagine tracing her temples and ears, caressing through them to the high-powered brain crunching her thoughts. As his gaze alighted on her sensuous neck, he knew she would be most wonderful to make love to, and he took every mental snapshot he could before she ever noticed his stare.

"They'll be great for sure, but with all that talking," Oskie said as he put his new photo album of Elly away and pictured the Taylor home soon to be plus one, "bless Boo's heart."

The two of them laughed in unison.

"Well, you're a coach too, mister," she retorted. "How does Turbo handle all your stories?"

"It is nice to have a captive audience sometimes, I guess." Oskie conceded his chattiness but wouldn't take all the credit. "I think coaches, teachers, lawyers, even social workers like you, all the talking professions, like to believe if they talk enough, they just might say something extraordinary that makes a difference.

"But I made a pact with Turbo, trying never to be like Charlie Brown's teacher. I'm his dad twenty-four seven and am there for anything he asks. But for practices and games, I try let people like D coach him, and I coach everyone else. Too much of the same voice can get tuned out.

"I don't imagine you've turned into a rabid cheer mom with Leigh?"

Elly cackled at the notion, and her spontaneous, adorable response sent a tickle through Oskie, one he could identify only as the warm, fuzzy feeling he got from his favorite chai tea.

"Lawl," as Elly let her inner Kentucky out, "I'm moral support only, unless she ever drops her pom-poms for a basketball. Scored two thousand points and have a daughter that can't dribble and chew gum. I sure don't have enough coaching in me to fix that!" She was still laughing.

"Speaking of basketball, take a gander over there." Elly pointed out the arena in the nearby skyline and ducked the car into a parking garage.

The game altered the date's dynamic from conversational to physical. Walking in, Oskie weighed the distance close enough to smell the fragrance of her skin and far enough to still see the curves of her hips. A close game ensued, and they stood or sat or screamed, but all the while he stole unseen seconds to study every molecule that made her. Elly quivered during a late-game free throw, as if she were still playing and taking the important shot herself, and Oskie quivered when she grabbed his hand to steady herself as the shot went in. Then came overtime, granting more minutes in a seat beside her, and though Oskie had predicted a Kentucky win beforehand and they did indeed end up with more points, it felt like all the winning was his.

"Hold up!

Elly screamed and was springing through the crowd to the exits, pulling Oskie by the hand. She dodged a line of fans and darted across the concourse to an ice cream stand, which was about to close.

"You gotta have this. Best. Ice cream. Ever. Promise." She dragged out the words for effect. "Seriously, dude, this stuff is world famous! I had this in high school whenever we'd come to the state tournament here. Was my annual treat." She was genuinely joyous as she handed a cone to Oskie. "Wanna race?"

Oskie scoffed, as if to say both *Are you serious?* and *Please, woman! You're outside your mind if you think you can beat me.*

"Have at it, sister. Let's go!"

And the two dug in industriously while walking to the car. There were some smudges of cream on their noses and cheeks, but the ice cream was devoured far too fast for any to drip on their hands. Oskie laughed while launching the last of his cone into his mouth. She still had several bites to go, and though he helped wipe her face as a good sport, he could tell her disappointment was kind of real. She had been raised on competition too, and the stakes, no matter how small or tasty or fun, didn't matter.

"Hey, I shoulda warned you. I *never* lose at ice cream. D-Tay and Turbo both admit I'm weirdly skilled at such."

Elly chuckled again, bending over not to laugh the last of the cone up her nose. "Well, get this. I thought *I* was being sneaky. Leigh and all her friends consider me unbeatable too. Hard to believe that the two ice cream champs of Wilmington had never met up for a contest, eh?"

There were so many things going through Oskie's mind that were hard to believe. He struggled to process it all on the drive home. Her beauty, her humor, the competition, even the ice cream—she was enchanting to all his senses. Was there *nothing* wrong with her? And how, when he could find no imperfections, could she somehow be more lovely and charming *every* time he saw her? He had suspected he could love her at the courthouse just five days ago, and now four visits later, she had warmed his heart to bubbling over, such that the steam from the heat had obscured every other fan at the game. He had seen no one, absolutely *no one*, in a sea of thousands but her. Was this how they said love melted a man?

Darkness fell on their return drive, and in a silent moment, Oskie reopened his phone and the earlier e-mail from D-Tay, thinking he would post him an update. But D as usual had said enough for both of them. After the initial all-capped warning to stay focused on Elly, the e-mail offered,

> My only advice: When you know, you know. Don't overthink it.

And then, putting it into "three things," the way Hollis always liked to, D-Tay wrote,

> So it's 1) don't let this distract from your date, 2) don't overthink, and for 3) since limericks were good enough for Hollis, here ya go:

> I ask you not to think but feel instead.
> Please see that it's not hard, just like I said.

> Be any ghost; it's not a crime,
> But catch Ms. Pac-Man one damn time.

> You are worthy of more. Keep that in your head.

Oskie had openly absorbed the events of the day, included D-Tay's heartfelt encouragement, and the ardor stirred by Elly had overwhelmed him. He could feel the plane of his heart taking off. But how could the issue not warrant at least some intellectual debate? Shouldn't he at least explore the possible destination? If this was his *Miracle on 34th Street*, if this was to prove that real love (in place of Santa) existed and was for him, how could this trial of the century go off without at least some witnesses or argument? He had D-Tay's testimony, and he knew Belle believed he and Elly were similar souls who would be lucky to have each other. But he had an extra ninety minutes heading past St. Vincent's all the way to Wilmington, and he mulled in that time whether to delve into the positions of the protagonists themselves.

His thoughts on Elly rolled in furiously. She was the most astonishing of girls, easy to talk to and fun to be around. A good listener, kind and considerate, with the most infectious laugh he had ever heard. This girl was robust, refined, and real all at once, the kind of beauty and poise that rose above any circumstance; it was just there. Quite simply, he was looking at the sweetest, smartest, and sexiest woman he had ever seen, all in one package, sitting two feet away from him, and he had known it instantly. He could love her anew and yet as if he always had. As D-Tay put it, "When you know, you know."

Yes, the prosecution's case was fierce, but the defense had the benefit of precedent. After all, the plane of Oskie's heart had never landed on the isle of true love. It had always crashed and burned, usually due to pilot error. Yes, the spark of love was new and fun, but how would Elly fare when Oskie's thought traps grabbed her and pulled her down, when he woke up determined to be disinterested while trying to choke emotion—and her—out of his life? Or when he remembered he hadn't lived a life deserving of such luck or joy, and that the very thought of that unworthiness, the lack of gratitude for Elly's affection, would render Oskie that much more unworthy? The defense was right. Oskie's mind would try to trample over his heart or have it framed as a fraud.

And thus became the comedy of Oskie's first kiss from Elly, the last first kiss he intended to ever have. By the time Elly pulled them into Oskie's driveway, somewhere around ten p.m., Oskie had reached his verdict to give up. In a deluded sense of self-righteousness and martyrdom, he couldn't digest the potential harm to Elly. She was too precious to be polluted by his inevitable plane crash. No way she heard all this baggage and still wanted him anyway.

So they sat there in her car, faces inches apart, while Oskie emptied out every thought in his head. All of it ... just as he had thought it through on the way home. But somewhere in the trial's play by play, just after Oskie let loose the stirrings in his heart but before he could ruin it with the reasons in his brain, Elly pounced. She had drifted closer, slowly, thinking him cuter and more lovable with every word, until they were nose to nose, even as he rambled on unaware, hell bent on saving them from destruction. Instead, ironically without one word, Elly did all the saving with a kiss.

She overcame Oskie with sensation, and he could literally feel her love through her lips. It obliterated all his thoughts, leaving him with the spellbinding allure of her gentle sounds and smell and skin. He had never wanted more eyes, some to close while lost in her sensuous kiss and some to open to record her every move—or more hands to feel every inch of her simultaneously.

Very few people know how or why a first kiss ends, at least for those kisses of true love, because the concept of time ceases to exist in that dimension. In fact, real lovers can recreate those kisses in their mind's eye at a moment's notice so vividly; it's as if that first kiss never ended at all.

Oskie stood there in his driveway, still kissing Elly even as she drove away, able to nail down only two other things: he adored her, and she had no holes whatsoever.

— 19 —

Hope You Hear

Oskie had never met a lazy Sunday morning he didn't like. But a lazy Sunday morning after falling in love was his new Christmas. He was walking CP when he opened his first gift, a text from Elly.

Elly	Oskie
Hey	
	Yes, ma'am?
Three thoughts on last night. Ready?	
	Go for it.
You're better at ice cream than me.	
	My mouth is bigger. ☺
Maybe that explains #2 too!	
	Gimme that again??
When a woman is in your face	

wanting a kiss,
that's NOT the
time to tell her why
she shouldn't!

Haha! Sorry. ☺
Promise I tried to shut up.

I'd like to do it again.

...

And I know you know.
I just have to say it.

You already know.
I do too. ☺

That she naturally spoke in threes, like Oskie had learned from Hollis, could have been coincidence. That she had used it to inspire Oskie toward love—and laughter—at the same time? That was the lottery equivalent of Oskie discovering a new moon and then being the only one chosen to land on it.

The phone buzzed in another text but not from Elly; it was Linda Baker with, "Dylan, I have a pretty solid offer on the house. Would you like to meet at Second Street today to discuss? We can go over the terms and maybe a timeline to get everything cleared out. Would one thirty work?"

Oskie pocketed the phone and ran his hand through his bedhead, the other hand still hanging on to CP's leash. CP had ceased all business and had chosen a prime piece of grass to sit and enjoy the brisk February breeze that morning.

"Well, CP … guess we can't be lazy *all* day."

CP turned his head in indifference, reminding the world, *I'm the king 'round here.* But then he scurried toward the front door to greet a sleepy Turbo, who was still rubbing his eyes and trying to be human as he came outside.

"Good morning, sir. Sleep okay?"

Turbo nodded slowly as he sat down on the porch steps to give CP the rubdown he desired. Those two loved lazy Sundays too. Oskie sat down beside them and recognized how grateful he was to have them both.

"We don't have much today, but we do have to go over to Grandpa's house in a bit. You remember Ms. Linda?"

Turbo restarted his nodding, still unable to manipulate his mouth for words.

"Well, looks like she's gotten Grandpa's house sold. Just might need you to go through your stuff over there and pick out what you'd like to keep and bring over here, and the rest of it we can give to Goodwill."

Turbo had CP in blissful submission, reaching all the places paws couldn't.

"Dad, where do you think he is? Where do people go when they die? Doesn't Grandpa's spirit need his house?"

Oskie almost laughed aloud and would have but for the depth of the question. A parent is never off duty, even when he or she may have just fallen in love.

"That is a *great* question, sir. Let's see if some eggs can help us figure it out."

Oskie started the threesome toward the kitchen, wondering where parents go when they don't have all the answers.

"C'mon in! I'm in the kitchen!"

Linda yelled from inside the Second Street house as Oskie and Turbo approached the front stoop. She had propped open the screen door to air out the stale. Three kids tossing football caught their attention from the house across the street.

"That be okay?" Turbo saw visions of two on two.

"Yes, sir. Just nowhere else unless you ask. Got it?"

"Promise!" An agreement made with Turbo already halfway there.

Oskie found Linda sorting through a mix of the usual legal documents and real estate checklists covering the kitchen table.

"Whoa there, my lady." They were usual to Linda but looked ominous to Oskie. "Anything I can help you with?"

"Oh, it's nothing, Dylan. Just disclosures and such. Really just need those and the contracts signed. That's the most important for now. I got hold of Belle too. She's on her way to sign and get some things."

She watched him survey the perimeter of the kitchen window.

"Guess I should be asking you the same thing? If I can help *you*? You know I've done this before, right?"

She looked up at him as he looked back at her, and though their eyes sold comfort, both of their memories delivered pain. Oskie flashed back to the last time he had sat in that kitchen with Linda, listening to her discuss Hollis's planned eulogy for Pookie's funeral. In return, Linda's vision actually saw Pookie himself, in the form of Oskie, molding his face into what she imagined her son would have looked like at that age.

"It can be hard deciding what of them to keep and what of them to let go." Her voice rose from experience both acquired and ongoing.

"I'm sorry, Aunt Linda." Faced with the plight of putting away Hollis's life, Oskie registered the full burden she had pushed through with Pookie. "I haven't quite helped you much these past ten years."

"Now, now ... I should be the one apologizing, Dylan." Linda refused to let him carry her weight. "Zack really made it hard on the both of us, didn't he? I was drowning in sorrow, Dylan. I knew you were too, but I could barely save myself back then. I knew you needed distance, even if just down the street."

The two let silence distill the words to their true meaning, as it always did. She had worried for Oskie since Pookie's death, but at least she had known he was near and safe back in Wilmington. She had saved herself from the sadness since then without Oskie's help, and she longed to know he had done the same.

"You always had questions, Dylan. Always needed a *why*. That was really the biggest difference in you and Zack. He felt things first, thought about them later, and you were the opposite, like two parts of the same superhero."

Linda tried truth laced with levity. The subject of a suicide was forever sensitive. "If only Pookie's fame had drug its feet some maybe. It just felt so good to him. He got so high. But when those questions finally hit him—those same questions you have—the world was clearly not what he imagined it to be. He had no gravity, and the fall was more than he could stand."

"I still should have been there for him." That was all Oskie could muster before his words wobbled.

"Don't, my child."

Her motherly instinct needed to get this out of him but also reacted to cut off his hurt. "You *were* there for him. We all were. But Zack chose to keep his head in the sand about life. No matter how easy the self-deception is and no matter how good it feels, not making a decision is actually making one. His life should have far outlasted his sports talent and notoriety, but he just couldn't—or sadly wouldn't—distinguish the two. We are all fools and cowards sometimes, and God rest his soul, we are sometimes both."

She acknowledged the tough love coming out of her heart, but they all three needed the therapy. It had been ten years overdue.

"Point being, Dylan, we didn't lose him. He lost himself. And I just don't want that to happen to you too. It just can't." Her voice cracked a bit. "Come here a second. Let me show you something."

She walked him to the front room of the house, and like Hollis in the middle of a coaching speech, she grew emboldened on the way. "You know what every parent wants over everything else?"

She answered her own rhetorical question with a visual aid. "That!" She pointed to the corner cake photo in the center of Hollis's trophy shelves, the one with Oskie at full smile while mucking it up with his best friends. "A parent wants to see their child joyful with himself and sharing that joy, engaged with the world, connected with his family and friends. That's what I see in that picture. That's what made it Hollis's favorite. He didn't want a thank-you or a pat on the back or any silly award for raising you. He wanted what he saw in that picture.

"I know we've never really talked about all this, Dylan. But your dad was no different than the rest of us. Same questions. Same desire for all his days on this earth to amount to something. That it wasn't for naught. And it wasn't Annie's death or Pookie's death or the legal system or the town's gossip column or a big sports loss that left him a ghost on his bad days. It wasn't being able to answer those questions for *you*. Of all he did, being your dad was the job he wanted most, the one he put the most sweat into, but he just couldn't make you whole during your nomadic years after your mom died. He knew you had to find your own answers. We all do. But it was hard for him not to feel like a failure."

"Uhhhh … did I come at a bad time?" Belle poked her smiling face in the propped-open screen door. Neither Linda nor Oskie knew how long she had been there, but judging from her next statement, she had heard the whole thing.

"No need to fret with me, okay." She talked fast, not wanting to interrupt. "I have no idea about selling any houses, so just let me know what to sign and when. And I will stop by one day this week to get anything I might want to keep. I just came on by today for Turbo. Can he come on home with me? His uncle needs a lesson in John Madden."

"And *FIFA* too!"

The soccer add on came from Turbo's head cresting with a huge smile between the doorframe and Belle's belly. They looked like a Dr.

Seuss book with Thing One smiling under *The Cat in the Hat*. Oskie could only smile back and shake his head.

"Done deal then. I'll bring him to you later. No worries. Just text me what I need to know on the house. And thank you, Linda."

Their heads vanished, and Oskie went to release the screen door shut. The February chill had softened the aroma of the house, just as Belle's disruption seemed to have softened Linda's love.

"Let me show you just one more thing, okay?"

Linda pulled a Post-it note from her purse and handed it to Oskie. "I didn't know about the book of limericks until last Sunday, but your dad had written that one and showed me years ago, when you were overseas. I spotted and copied it down while you were watching the Super Bowl.

> [Journal Page 69, Linda's Favorite]
>
> When I'm gone from this place, would you learn from me then?
> Will you get warmth from my pace when my candle ends?
>
> Let your soul heal its break, if you hear nothing I've said.
> You have my heart to take, even when my body's dead.
>
> I have shared and hope you hear; up to you on when.

"Those could just as easily be words from me or your mom or Zack or anyone who loves you. It's pretty simple, Dylan. You can make peace for all of us by making peace for yourself."

"Hey now!"

D-Tay bounced into Newberry's around six p.m. that evening, finding Oskie already in their usual booth. Oskie had mopped up a real estate plan with Linda and, sans Turbo for the evening, made his way to their Sunday evening café early.

"Tell me something new, sir!"

Oskie tried to surmise which of his last twenty-four hours D would dive into first.

"Hmmmmm … lot of moving pieces in the last day or so, doncha think? Let's start with this. Can we move tomorrow morning's practice back a day? There's a really good chance Boo comes home with me from court tomorrow, and it would be flat-out awesome if he could come to practice the next morning. If you agree, I promise I'll tell all the parents of the change so you won't have to."

"Agreed, sir. That's an easy one. What else ya got?"

Oskie knew D had other questions, and unlike the car ride yesterday, he was feeling fairly frisky and ready to answer them.

"You know what, man …" D used perfect sign language slang to order two milkshakes from Laverne, who was standing at the counter, hoping he would save her the trip over. "I'm not gonna ask you any details at all. You know I'm happy for you, I'm proud of you, and most of all, you need to know I trust you to do the right thing for yourself.

"Whatever you're feeling, just be a good quarterback and don't beat yourself in this game for once. Whatever you find with Elly, love or friendship or fun, don't ever take the easy way out once you have it. And like Laverne told us last week"—again he perfectly timed a nod and a thumbs-up as Laverne dropped off the shakes—"don't let anything outside of the two of you blow out the candle you create.

"Like your dad used to say, 'Integrity stays true even when the sky is falling,' so even when you feel jaded or that the selfishness in this world outnumbers us, don't let it turn you into selfish when it comes to her. Share *everything* with her and trust that she needs exactly that.

"Be defiant. Be that guy I've always known that hates to lose more than anyone. Forbid the world to enter into your inner circle. Not inside your hearts. That's the good stuff only for the two of you. You think anything could tear me away from Mary Beth? Hell, naw."

D's fervor overwhelmed him, contorting his pep talk for Oskie's beginning relationship into an emotional reminder and affirmation of his own true love. They cut the weekly coach's meeting short and took the shakes to go, because D wanted to go straight home and kiss his wife.

— 20 —

NEWLY PROCLAIMED FREEDOM

D's early departure left Oskie his Sunday evening home alone with CP. He decided to make himself what he called a Mike Ditka, basically a screwdriver disguised in a coffee mug, and to take CP on a long walk to recap the week that had been.

Just seven days ago, Hollis's house needed to be sold, Boo still lived in the Fairview housing projects, Linda had never talked openly about Pookie's death, and D-Tay, to anyone's knowledge, had never written a limerick. Oh yeah, and Oskie hadn't had a date in a year. Throw in the Patriots winning the Super Bowl and Kentucky toppling Louisville, and it had been a hell of a week.

Oskie thought back to the navy pilots he had heard during transport days for his National Guard duty. He could hear them on the radio. "Visors down, full throttle, release brakes, we are rollin'." Maybe it was the vodka sips as he walked the roads of Whitemarsh with CP, or maybe it was D-Tay's fire-and-brimstone exhortation at the coffee shop, but full throttle was the way his life felt, leaving the question of the day. What was he prepared to do about it? So many of those pilots had talked of their knees shakin' in fear as the planes roared up and rolled to their course, and if you asked fifty of them, you would have gotten fifty different answers on how they sustained their courage to get through it. Some said pride, the shame of failure, religion, or even some old coaching lesson or philosophy imparted years before. Of course, some ran away.

CP was sniffing a mailbox, likely the thousandth time he had inspected that same mailbox, never once questioning his motivation or mission in doing so. Oskie was simultaneously frustrated CP wouldn't keep walking and jealous of his confident resolve.

"That's it!" Oskie giggled to himself while taking another swig of liquor. "I'm going to figure out my personal philosophy once and for all. I don't care if I have to get drunk and stay up all night like Edgar Allan Poe—well, maybe minus the cocaine and strange bird on the wall. I'm going to outline the basic programming of my decision-making process. It's like coaching kids. They learn in building blocks. You polish up their most basic skills and steps that then combine into the larger concepts and strategies. But even before they can perfect the drills, they must learn how to learn. And they do that by adhering to a few simple constants, eyes up, hands still, and mouths closed while the coach is talking, for example. Things we accept as true always, whether you're alone in a gym or performing under pressure with the world watching.

"I'm about to carve out Oskie's building blocks of life. I'm freakin' forty, CP! I'd say it's time I tried to learn how to live.

"*Enough* of this eternal, exhausting consternation. Either I decide to do something and have the courage and conviction to see it through, knowing the exact rationale upon which I act, or I decide not to do something, and I leave it behind with equal clarity and certainty, having no regrets. I need to set down rules to help me do that. This quarter life or midlife crisis, with the weak ass, pointless drifting, and the inability to assert control stops tonight!

"Ya know what, CP?" Oskie had now joined most adults in always giving their best speeches in the shower or while driving or walking their dogs. "This dog walk marks the *last* time I am a product of my past or my surroundings. I refuse to let the past render me guilty as a failure or anxiously to blame for everyone else's setbacks. I am not some Sisyphus resigned to pushing rocks on some gray line of mediocrity. Who the hell is calling it mediocre, and who the hell put me on that line? You're looking at him. My career is not really gray and not really mediocre, and if it was, I should get the hell out of it.

"And I'm ashamed to say this, CP, so keep this under your ears, but I had heard, believed, and even repeated that old fence post story, that you can remove the nails and even paint over it, but the holes from the nails are still there, just like the hurts of the past allegedly never go away. CP! That's *complete* trash! Forget that freakin' fence post. What's wrong with getting off my ass and building a whole new fence?

"I'm in, CP! I'm gonna stay here and build that damn fence. For me, for Turbo, for you, for Elly if she wants … I'm not gonna be one of those running-away pilots. You can't run from your past, and you damn sure can't run from yourself. I've tried that on three continents.

"And peep this. We're gonna build *our* fence *our* way, not according to anyone else's view. All the pundits and their proverbs mean nothing anyway if it's not personal to us. I've tried both extremes, CP … from predestination and 'Everything happens for a reason' to full free will and control, as in 'You can do anything you set your mind to' or 'Strong men don't believe in luck but in cause and effect.' But it is *all* relative. Those axioms are great if they fit your personal tragedy or religion or selfishness or position of affluence. But you won't ever hear a homeless guy on the corner, a starving kid in the third world, or even Boo at St. Vincent's, ever claiming those theories.

"Look, pup, I'm not advocating self-pity when things are bad. I agree that no one is coming to save you, so you save yourself if at all possible. I understand the socioeconomic heist going on all around us, the greed and inequalities all over, and I'm fine with my cut, and what I can make of it, even with the millions of others who have more or less simply because of random chance in most cases. But what I'm saying… what I intend to solve for myself, once and for all, is the *reason* behind the whole show and *why* I want to be in it. You get all that, big man?"

The walk had slowed to a halt, and CP chose that moment to take a dump, either in honor of, or simply on top of, all Oskie's rant. In alignment with his newly proclaimed freedom, Oskie chose to take the defecation as a positive omen and laughed with CP on a post-poo sprint back to the house.

Oskie couldn't wait to sketch out his thoughts, part in words and part in pictures streaming across his mind's eye so fast he was afraid they would slip by before he could get them on paper. He had always been a better writer than talker, as perhaps Elly on their date and definitely CP on their walk had now found out the hard way.

Oskie grabbed a pen and stationery and decided to compose a letter to his parents, since they had helped form a large portion of his theories, and then he would store the letter as a time capsule for a year. Tomorrow, February 10, would be his New Year's Day. He would adopt his resolutions and see where his world stood in twelve months, and he couldn't remember being so excited to start a new year.

February 9

Dear Mom & Dad,

I miss you, and I love you. I hope that's a given for both of you, down to your souls.

As of today, know that your son is even. Everything in my life to this point. I'm resetting the score to 0–0. For every Simpson kid I help in juvenile court, there's a Ditters I couldn't. For every adoring fan of my achievement, I can show you an equally enthusiastic hater. For every D-Tay who keeps me close, there's a Pookie who left me behind. These are the things I've seen in forty years of life. It's all even. Everything means something, and at the same time, nothing does. Dealing with that dilemma is life's ultimate question.

I do not yet have an answer to that question or so many others. I know enough only to know I do not know anything, other than that there will always be questions on life's journey, for both parents and their children, and some will go unanswered. I believe though that the absence of answers is not permission to stop. In fact, it is motivation to keep moving forward, to solve as many of those questions as possible before the clock of life ticks down.

Life really is like a game, which I know you both can appreciate. Though day after day life may seem like the same game, with a preordained outcome, there is always still the possibility that your team—your family—and the love you invest in them will rise to something extraordinary and maybe even reach one of those answers we all seek. We never know when or even if those moments come, but they definitely *never* come without a heart's full commitment. You have to have a vision and believe it is possible, you have to give everything you have in working toward it, and you have to find joy in the process and share it along the way. I will admit that Dad's three bones—wishbone, backbone, and funny bone—make the most sense of anything I have heard.

So going forward, to make sure I stay fully engaged, I am going to lay out the answers I have found so far, the directions to which you laid out for me. To pay Dad back for the bones, I will make it three. ☺

1. Empathy is worth it, and I will do my part. Dad, I struggled with this one, but I had it wrong. We are not chameleons carrying the weight of others out of duty, just shifting through life to please parents, then a spouse, then children, or those who praise us. That only surrenders ownership of your own life, rendering it meaningless. We invest our hearts in others to share and reinforce our hope, that which keeps us all afloat. Conjoined hearts provide the chance for greatness you can never get alone, like a team, and the world needs its good hearts. The world is still worth fighting for, and we cannot let *them*, as Judge Pete says, outnumber *us*.

2. Love is real, and I am going to offer it the right way. I slipped this in the middle to see if you are paying attention. Again, I had it wrong. I had dismissed love as a made-up antidote to loneliness, emotions used as a pretense to keep a companion on a life to nowhere. That is all an outsider to *real* love can see, and there is no changing that perspective except by finding it, by being on the inside of someone else's heart, by actually feeling it through their words and lips and fingers. It is a miraculous candle ignited between two people outside of any timing or planning, and if you fail to act, the flame dies, and love moves elsewhere. If given the chance, that will *not* be me for once. I will be *all in*. Wherever it leads. I shall love as hard

as a man can every day, yet it will not be *work*, just limitless desire inspired by her presence.

3. Family never leaves you, and I will keep your lessons in my heart. Turbo just asked this question this morning, wondering where we all go when we die. I have asked a similar question in a different way for years, a little voice inside my head saying, "What's the point?" I think with families, both those you are born to and those you acquire along life's way, this is the point: All the stories, lessons, experiences, and emotions accumulate and pass on ... everything we give and gather ... and those heart-shaped libraries from the ones before help those of us that follow. That is how families survive intact. It is not all for naught.

I want you to have peace now, as I do, not in that I have all the answers but that I am excited to go after them, and I know I will find my adventure and happiness along the way.

Yours Always,
Oskie

Oskie was just folding and stuffing his letter when car lights stopped in the window facing the front yard. He opened the door, and CP ran out, recognizing the car and, most merrily, Turbo's silhouette now coming up the driveway. Turbo paused for a hug from his father before taking the pup back inside to prep for bed. Oskie, now in the same baggy sweats he had started with on this lazy Sunday, made his way toward Belle, who was sitting in the driver's seat with the car still running.

"Was he good for you, sis?"

"Always is, *Booas*. Turbo's the best. If you ever decide to get rid of him, call me first."

She meant it lightheartedly, her usual self. It was just a usual babysitting drop-off, but Oskie lingered at the car window. She noticed his stillness.

"Thank you, Belle. You're always sweet to me, and I'm lucky to have you."

She tried to put her finger on the difference in his words, and she couldn't see the color of his eyes in the shadows of the street lights, but she could feel his gaze on her. He was heavier somehow, as if rooted where he stood.

"Belle, if you ever need anything, I want you to let me help you sometime. If you need me to watch the kids, if you need money, whatever I could help with, okay? I'm grateful for you, and it would be nice to show it for a change."

"Of course, Bub." She was rarely caught off guard as her mind ran through the possibilities … his date with Elly … maybe the afternoon with Linda … but she had no way of knowing the explosion in his mind over the last hour. "I'll talk to you tomorrow, okay? We'll plan a get-together, promise." She patted his hand, which still hung on the car door. "You know I love you."

"I love you, too."

She drove off slowly, trying to compute the change she felt from him. His voice had sounded unburdened, his concern so heartfelt. She decided to describe his words as pure, unfettered by his longstanding fog; or even better, she had witnessed him at peace.

〜

EPILOGUE

Oskie hopped up from Linda's long dining table to grab the last dessert from the stove. Not necessarily because of any need, since there were ample sources of diabetes already on display that Saturday afternoon, but more because he was just happy and wanted to move. Oskie noticed the calendar on the refrigerator said August 22, 8–22, incidentally his favorite two numbers. *Poetic*, he thought.

The first annual Baker family celebration had been a huge success, and though that sounded cliché, both of those adjectives were intentional and appropriate. First, the *success*! Six months after acquiring temporary custody, D-Tay and Mary Beth had finalized their permanent adoption of Boo, who was now a bit fatter, a whole lot happier, and most importantly, well-adjusted and comfortable eating Cheez-Its and playing video games with Turbo in the playroom at the other end of the house.

Just a week prior to that, Turbo, Boo, and company had finished their travel baseball team summer circuit, taking the ten-and-under state title. The dog day heat and stress had evaporated about ten pounds off Oskie and D each, perhaps to the unspoken delight of Elly and Mary Beth respectively. In turn, the ladies busied themselves looking for the ten pounds the men had lost, which they appeared to think would be in the Oreo chocolate chip ice cream cake centered between them. Mary Beth's brother Stephen, already status post two desserts, was lurking quietly to help them with any stray sweets they had missed.

"Pardon me, sir, but you're not going to hog that apple pie, are you?" Judge Pete broke Oskie's mental survey of the room with his usual wit. "Some of us are dying sooner than others over here."

Oskie scrambled to attention and handed the pie over to Judge Peterson and his wife as well as Ronny, all of whom had ridden together. "By all means, *Dr.* Peterson. It's all yours, unless the ladies want to fight you for it.

"Dr., eh?" Pete rolled his eyes. "I know I have a JD, but your flattery makes me suspicious, sir."

"'When in doubt, always crown,' a wise man once told me."

Oskie knew Pete would get the Hollis reference, and Pete nodded his nonverbal, *Nice one*, while digging into the pie.

The only one not eating was CP, snugly curled up asleep in the lap of Leigh, who was fast gaining on Turbo as CP's best friend.

And that brings us to the *huge*. Linda Baker, she of the emptying nest just six months ago, was sitting atop a table honoring her family of now thirteen! Oskie stood propped in the kitchen archway and took measure of her for a moment. Linda's life had changed almost as much as his had in the past six months. Meanwhile, Oskie was still keeping his resolutions, and he was still asking himself the questions of the day.

Did Linda have any idea that her family would grow so large?

Did D and Mary Beth know they would have a son in their charge?

Did Elly know she shone like the sun?

Did she know Oskie would circle her like every planet in one?

Did Turbo know he hadn't lost a teammate but gained a brother?

Did Turbo plan on a sister (Oskie hadn't asked Elly yet but may one day or another)?

Did Pete and Ronny expect their loyalty and kindness to win?

Did they appreciate more the desserts or Oskie's every last grin?

There were all sorts of those questions, as there were *always* questions for Oskie's brain to bake.

He would have said no to all of them six months ago, but today, yes, they were all his corner cake.

Speaking of cake … Oskie hovered with his questions but still had his priorities, and he had navigated himself neatly in front of the perfect remaining corner of the ice cream cake. Patience and poise, even the occasional misdirection, over two hours of focus invested to get to the best part of the meal. You want it first, but you save it for last, so that when it comes, if it survives, it will be its best self, the best piece. Just for you.

Hold up. He had to drop his fork just as he was about to bite. He had an answer! It had to come out before he lost it. He grabbed the cake (priorities remember?) and slipped quietly to the empty kitchen, scribbling his thoughts and attaching the following Post-it note to Linda's refrigerator:

[Linda's Fridge]

What lies ahead for all of us, there is just no way to know.
You hold hope to find the point of this, a compass as you grow.

This life is not easy. Your heart can freeze.
But if you try, the juice is worth the squeeze.

You can find love, joy, and corner cake, and *that is why you go!*

CPSIA information can be obtained
at www.ICGtesting.com
Printed in the USA
BVHW081327301120
594475BV00004B/591

9 781480 894198